The Strongest Passion

by

Luis Zapata

Translated by Clary Loisel, Ph.D.

Floricanto Press

ISBN: 978-0-915745-76-0

Floricanto Press
650 Castro Street, Suite 120-331
Mountain View, California 94041-2055
www.floricantopress.com

The Strongest Passion

For Joaquín

One

I

"Hello."

"Arturo?"

"Yeah, who's calling?"

"Santiago. Do you remember me?"

"Come on, don't be silly—we saw each other just last week."

"Well, it's just that..."

"It's taken you a while to call, hasn't it?"

"What do you mean?"

"I thought you were going to call sooner."

"Why?"

"Well, because you were supposed to call. Didn't you tell my mother you were going to look into the business about the stocks?"

"Uh, well yes, but..."

"Did you want to talk to her? She's not here right now."

"I did not want to talk to her. I want to talk to you."

"Oh..."

"Are you busy?"

"No. Well, ah—I was working out."

"I'm not taking up too much of your time, am I?"

"Yeah, you are, but there's nothing to be done about it."

"Hey, you know you really have bad manners."

"So then what am I good for?"

"Oh boy...if I told you..."

"Tell me."

"I'll tell you later...when I trust you better."

"Why did you gulp?"

"What?"

"I said why did you gulp?"

"Don't be smart, Arturo."

"What were you thinking about?"

"That...it would be better if I told you later."

"When you trust me better?"

"Yes."

"Do you want me to tell my mother to call you?"

"No. No. Don't tell her anything. If I called it was because I wanted to talk to you—I just told you that. Besides, I'm not in Mexico City."

"Where are you?"

"Guess."

"Are you in the country?"

"No."

"Well then...in San Francisco."

"No."

"In New York."

"No."

"In Chicago."

"Wrong again."

"Are you in the U.S.?"

"Yes."

"In Brownsville. You went to smuggle something back into Mexico."

"You're right about the smuggling but not about where I am."

"Did you really go to the U.S. to try to smuggle something back into Mexico?"

"Well, no. I'm tying up some business matters, but..."

"Do you have a house there?"

"Yes, but I also..."

"That's cool."

"I was also going to tell you I found time to buy you something."

"Really?"

"Yes..."

"What is it, huh?"

"It's going to be a surprise."

"Tell me what it is."

"You should get it by tomorrow."

"You're not going to give it to me in person?"

"No."

"Don't be a coward, Santiago."

"Why do you say 'coward'?"

"Because you don't want to give it to me in person."

"When I see you, I'll give you another present. What I sent you is just to give you a taste of what's in store for you, but I wanted it to be in your hands as soon as possible."

"Well, thanks, but why?"

"Because I saw it, and it made me think of you. I thought you'd like it. I'm also sending a gift to your mother."

"To throw her off track?"

"What do you mean to throw her off track? What's wrong with sending you a gift? What's so strange about that?"

"There's nothing strange...it's just that you're sending something to my mother as well."

"Listen to me—you want to know why? It's because I really care about your mother..."

"You're not shy at all, are you?"

"No. Is that bad?"

"You can't divide everything into good and bad, can you?"

"I don't know."

"Look Arturo...I haven't been able to sleep lately. Since I saw you the other day, I haven't been able to sleep. And last night was the..."

"You gulped again."

"It's just that you make me nervous. Who would believe it...that at my age..."

"Why do I make you nervous?"

"For a lot of reasons."

"Such as?"

"Because you're very handsome."

"What else?"

"Also because you're very young."

"And what's that got to do with anything?"

"I don't know, but that's another reason why you make me nervous."

"How weird—you're my mother's only friend who gets nervous about those things."

"Well I..."

"What else makes you nervous, huh?"

"Well...when I think about..."

"Don't gulp anymore, man."

"You're making fun of me, aren't you?"

"Well, go on."

"It makes me nervous to think...to think we could become friends."

"Just friends?"

"Well, it's up to you. It depends on you."

"This call is going to cost you a fortune wherever you're calling from."

"I don't care."

"Really?"

"No."

"Then, you must have a lot of money, Little Ole Santiago."

"Don't call me Little Ole Santiago."

"Why not?"

"It makes me feel like you're making fun of me—again."

"Do you really think so?"

"Well are you?"

"It's with affection, man."

"You feel affection toward me?"

"Well, no, I don't because I still don't know you very well."

"What do you mean you don't know me?"

"Well, I know you, but I don't remember you."

"Then you're going to see more of me, to see if..."

"My mother is really quite fond of you, isn't she?"

"Yes."

"There you go. For me it's as if you were part of the family."

"Don't say that."

"Why not?"

"Because I want you to...I want you to like me for another reason. I'd like it that in our friendship, the ties I have with Sarita¹ don't have any bearing."

"Oh..."

"Why are you laughing?"

"I didn't laugh."

"Really?"

"Really."

"And do you have a girlfriend, Arturo?"

"Come on, Santiago."

"This time you laughed for sure. You can't deny it. How come?"

"Please Santiago."

"You think it's funny I'm asking you if you have a girlfriend?"

"Well, to be honest, yeah."

"Why?"

"Because it's not in style to have a girlfriend."

"Then what is in style? To have a boyfriend?"

"Not that either."

"Then what?"

"Nothing. If you like someone, you sleep with them, and that's it."

"It's that easy?"

"It's that easy."

"And do you have...do you have sex with many people?"

"No."

"Why not?"

"Because I don't. What about you?"

"Not me. I'm interested in more meaningful things."

"Like what?"

"You won't laugh if I tell you?"

"No."

"Really?"

"Really, man."

"Love, companionship, ..."

"Get real, Santiago."

"You see? You said you weren't going to laugh."

"Well, yeah, but it's just that you're so funny."

"What do you mean funny? How am I so funny?"

"You talk like in old movies."

"....."

"Are you angry I said that to you?"

"No. Why?"

"Then, why were you so quiet?"

"I was thinking."

"About?"

"About the many things that separate us—the many years in our ages...that you're from another generation."

"Oh."

"A very different and liberated generation—which I really like..."

"Me or my generation?"

"Both...look, when I was young..."

"Oh, come on!"

"Hey, hey, are you calling me old?"

"No, why do you say that?"

"Well, besides, what would be wrong if I am, huh?"

"Say, didn't you call a little while ago?"

"Me? No. At what time?"

"About a half hour ago."

"No. Why do you ask?"

"Because somebody called and hung up."

"And why do you think it was me?"

"Then who was it?"

"It could have been someone who misdialed, or...maybe it was a secret admirer who didn't have the nerve to talk to you."

"Exactly."

"Come on, Arturo. I have enough backbone to talk to you directly, don't you think? This call should be proving that to you."

"Well, maybe you just wanted to see who would answer, huh? You didn't want my mother to answer."

"If your mother had answered, I would have been happy to talk to her."

"Yeah, but you wouldn't have had the nerve to tell her you wanted to talk to me, would you?"

"Who knows?"

"See how you really don't have the backbone you say you do."

"That doesn't have anything to do with it—I just wouldn't have done it out of respect for Sarita. And in that case, I would have asked her to tell you hello for me and..."

"And you would have called back when she wasn't here, right?"

"Could be."

"Oh come on, Little Ole Santiago."

"What kind of exercise were you doing?"

"One that I read about in a magazine."

"But why? You don't need to work out."

"So I'm too built?"

"I wouldn't say it like that."

"Then, how would you say it?"

"I'd say you have a very proportioned body, very...and your...and your build is just right... It seems to me you've got a little bit of an ego, don't you?"

"Me? Yeah. Can you tell?"

"A little."

"How so?"

"Well, precisely because of your interest in working out when you don't need to. Working out isn't necessary at your age."

"And do you exercise?"

"Yes, of course. At my age you have to make an effort to keep looking good."

"Then you've got an ego also."

"I'd say it like this: once you reach a certain age, you have to take care of yourself so as not to offend others with your appearance. Let's just say you have to learn how to age gracefully."

"Well, it's the same thing."

"No, it's not the same—if you think about it carefully, it's an attitude that takes other people into account."

"But it's the same thing—you're worried about what others might think of you. You're worried about how others see you."

"I've already told you it's not the same."

"I'm sure you also get massages."

"Of course."

"And spend time in the sauna and everything."

"You guessed it."

"Do you have a sauna at your house?"

"Yes."

"At your house in Mexico City?"

"Yes."

"And a jacuzzi?"

"Yes."

"When are you going to invite me over?"

"Whenever you want."

"Really?"

"Of course."

"When you get back?"

"Sure."

"And when are you getting back?"

"In a week."

"Have you ever had surgery, Santiago?"

"Do you mean cosmetic surgery?"

"Yeah."

"No, why would you ask me such a thing?"

"What's wrong with that?"

"It's not that there's anything wrong with it, but it just seems to me..."

"I know a lot of guys who have had cosmetic surgery."

"But they look really bad, don't they? Their features are altered."

"It depends. I think it depends on the surgeon, don't you?"

"Well, I don't know, but I wouldn't like it."

"Not even if you needed it?"

"Do you think I need cosmetic surgery now? Do you think I need to look different?"

"I don't know. I don't remember."

"You don't remember me...what I look like?"

"Not very well."

"But we just saw each other."

"Maybe that's why, huh?"

"I don't know. That used to happen to me when I met someone I was really interested in. And you're making it happen to me now—I remember you, but vaguely. I don't really remember your features very well for example. Isn't it strange I remember what you looked like as a child better than as an..."

"So, you think I'm interested in you?"

"I don't know. I'm telling you what used to happen to me...what is happening to me."

"Um...listen, this call is really going to cost you a fortune. We've been talking to each other for quite a while. Let's talk again another day."

"I already told you not to worry about that."

"Well, it's just that I really should be going."

"Where? Didn't you tell me you were working out?"

"Yeah, but it's gotten late."

"You're not going to finish your workout?"

"I'm just saying it's gotten late."

"And where are you going if you don't mind my asking?"

"To see a friend. I'm sure she's waiting for me."

"A female friend?"

"What difference does that make?"

"Well, some young people talk about their male friends as 'she'."

"Well, I don't—that's something a tired old queen would do."

"Like me?"

"I didn't say that... Do you? Do you talk about your male friends as if they were female?"

"Sometimes."

"Little Ole Santiaga[2]."

"Hey, you've really got a lot of nerve."

"This time I really have to go, all right?"

"And when are we going to talk again?"

"Whenever you want. When you get back."

"Not until then? I can call you before that. I'd like it if we talked some more."

"Fine. Just call me."

"When? When can you give me a little bit of your time?"

"See how funny you're talking?"

"All right already. When can I call you?"

"Well, when can you?"

"Whenever you want. May I call you tomorrow?"

"If you want."

"Then I'll talk to you tomorrow, all right? Behave yourself."

"O.K. See you later."

"I'll talk to you tomorrow, Arturo."

2

"Where did you go yesterday?"

"Me?"

"Yes. I called you, but you weren't home."

"Oh. And did you talk to my mother?"

"Yes, I took advantage of the opportunity to see how she was doing."

"Did you already check on the business about the stocks?"

"Yes."

"It seems you were disappointed she answered and not me."

"Truthfully, yes."

"And why is that, huh?"

"Because I was hoping to hear your voice."

"You should say, 'your sweet voice'."

"Your sweet voice. I was hoping to hear your sweet voice."

"I was just kidding, all right? But I see you took me seriously."

"But it's true—you do have a really nice voice."

"Yeah? What's so special about it?"

"It's pleasing, has a nice pitch, and it's masculine."

"Oh. And why were you disappointed when she answered?"

"I already told you—I was hoping to talk to you."

"It wouldn't be for some other reason, would it?"

"And what might that be?"

"Well, maybe because she suspects something."

"What? ...that I like you?"

"That you wanted to talk to me."

"I don't think that would bother her, would it?"

"Who knows? You know how she is. And so you really like me?"

"Yes, can't you tell?"

"A little bit. But don't you worry, all right? I won't tell her anything anyway."

"There wouldn't be anything wrong if you did."

"Well, but I'm giving you the peace of mind of knowing I'm not going to say anything."

"That's great, Arturo. That will make me trust you even more... Did you ever get your present?"

"Yeah."

"And did you like it?"

"Yeah. Thanks. Now I'm going to give you a present."

"Right now?"

"Yeah."

"Are you going to say you like me?"

"No. I'm going to tell you my mother is going away this weekend."

"And what does that have to do with anything?"

"You'll be able to call me more easily without having to be so careful."

"Hey, listen—I don't have to be careful of anyone. I'm an adult... And so where did you go yesterday?"

"To the movies."

"And what movie did you see?"

"Hey, Santiago, you sound like the police."

"Why do you say that? I'm not questioning you as if we were at an interrogation."

"Well, that's what it seems like."

"If I asked you about which movie you saw, it's because I'm interested in everything you do. I want to get to know you really well...I want to know about what you like, what you..."

"I went to see an old Hitchcock film."

"Those are really good, aren't they?"

"They're all right."

"Which one did you see?"

"Didn't I just tell you it was a Hitchcock film?"

"Yes, but which one?"

"I don't even remember the name. But I didn't like it... I thought it was really boring—nothing but a lot of talking and explanations."

"And who did you go with?"

"With a friend who's a girl—I want to make sure you understand. You're interrogating me again, don't you think?"

"Well, didn't we already agree this wasn't an interrogation?"

"You agreed to it."

"And that I really wanted to get to know you?"

"Well, that's what you say, but it seems to me you're a little underhanded—you change things so they suit you. You arrange everything so it turns out the way you want it."

"Hey, that's not true. I'm very sincere—if I said I wanted to get to know you, it was because that's how I felt. If not, I would've told you I liked interrogating or manipulating you..."

"Really?"

"Of course."

"And have you ever said that to anyone?"

"No, but..."

"You see? Didn't you just say you are very sincere?"

"Well, it's that I don't like to manipulate anybody. I think a romantic relationship or a friendship—whatever kind of relationship it is—should be based on equality and respect for the other person."

"That sounds like something from a history book."

"Well, what's in a history book also has its merit, don't you think? It's there for a reason."

"Oh, come on Santiago."

"How nice to hear my name when you say it."

"Santiago, Santiago, Santiago, Santiago, Santiago."

"No, I didn't like it like that—you said it as if you were making fun of me."

"I'm going to talk like you: 'Hey, that's not true.' I'm not making fun of you. I said it several ways to see which one you liked best."

"I liked the first time the best—when you said it without thinking."

"Oh."

"May I ask you some questions?"

"More?"

"These are more about what you like."

"Why do you want to know about that?"

"Well, because I already told you—I want to get to know you better."

"Sure. Go ahead."

"What is your favorite thing to do?"

"Travel."

"Have you traveled very much?"

"Not a lot—not as much as I'd like."

"The next time I take a trip, I'll take you along."

"Really?"

"Well, the next time I'll be taking a long trip. They aren't all that fun."

"Why not?"

"Because they're business trips—you'd get bored."

"So you have business abroad?"

"Houston really isn't abroad—Tijuana is farther away from Mexico City than Houston."

"Fine, but do you have business there?"

"Didn't we agree I would be the one asking the questions?"

"You agreed to that."

"But so did you."

"Whatever…next question?"

"What is your favorite flower?"

"The African magnolia."

"There's no such thing as the African magnolia."

"The German orchid."

"Again, there's no such thing. You're pulling my leg."

"Well then, the Dutch tulip. That one exists, doesn't it?"

"Yes. That's seriously your favorite flower?"

"Uh-huh."

"And your favorite food?"

"Hamburgers. Do you really think by asking me these kinds of questions you're going to get to know me better?"

"Of course. Everything has to do with the personality and the character of the person. A human being is like an enormous jigsaw puzzle, and the smallest piece—as insignificant as it might seem—tells you something about the whole."

"Ah. Later I'm going to ask you some questions, all right?"

"Yes, if you want… Let's see, how old were you when you

had your first sexual experience?"

"Oh, come on, don't be ridiculous. That kind of question doesn't count."

"Why not?"

"Because I said so."

"Are you embarrassed to talk about it?"

"I'm not embarrassed—I just don't want to tell you."

"Why not?"

"Because I just don't—end of story."

"Have you had much experience?"

"No, you?"

"Right now, I'm asking the questions. When it's your turn, I'll answer all the questions you want."

"O.K."

"Have you ever been in love?"

"No."

"You're that sure?"

"Yeah."

"But would you like to fall in love...?"

"It would depend who with."

"With someone who really loved you for example."

"Like you?"

"Yes."

"So you really love me a lot? That's impossible."

"Well, I...I like you a whole lot and..."

"Don't get nervous, man."

"I like you a lot, and I also believe I could come to love you. Do you think you could fall in love with me?"

"I don't know. It all depends."

"On what?"

"I don't know."

"...Well, what is the most important thing in the world to you?"

"I already told you—to travel."

"That's what you like more than anything else, right?"

"But it's also what's most important to me."

"I was talking about other kinds of things."

"Like what?"

"Your values, what you think is the most important goal to achieve in life."

"Well—to be happy."

"You're not happy?"

"No."

"What do you need to make you happy?"

"Wow, a lot of things."

"Tell me one."

"Money."

"Hey, come on, you already have a comfortable life."

"Well, you're asking me what I need—yes or no?"

"Yes, but...it seems to me you have everything you need."

"Well, look, I don't."

"Why do you need more money?"

"More money? I don't have any money. The person with the money is my mother."

"Fine, but what she has is yours also—it's for you. What would you need more for?"

"I already told you: to travel, to live by myself."

"Why do you want to live by yourself? Don't you have everything you need at your mother's house?"

"Man, Santiago, you don't understand."

"Yes, I do understand, of course I understand—don't think I don't. You lack a certain independence, a certain freedom of movement."

"Exactly."

"Sure, that's natural. You're at that age."

"I don't know, but those are definitely things I need."

"Don't worry, you'll get them."

"When I no longer need them..."

"Don't say that—it also depends on you to get what you want."

"Really?"

"Of course—it depends on whether or not you do something."

"Like kill my mother so I can inherit everything?"

"Hey, listen. Don't say such awful things."

"Then what can I do?"

"Work, toil..."

"Oh no, that's too much trouble."

"Then you don't really want it."

"So that's what you think?"

"What would you do if you had everything you needed?"

"I'd live really well—I'd travel a lot, I'd buy a lot of clothes for myself, I'd have a really fine car."

"You would certainly have a very active social life, and you would always be surrounded by friends, and you wouldn't do anything productive."

"Maybe."

"You see? That's why it's not good for you to have it all."

"So, do you have a lot of money, Santiago?"

"It's already your turn to ask questions?"

"Yeah, answer me: do you have a lot of money?"

"I think it would be better to say I have what's necessary."

"Necessary for what?"

"What's necessary to live comfortably, without fear, and to give a little bit of happiness to those around me."

"I see. And do you spend a lot?"

"Let's just say I don't like to skimp when it comes to giving myself a certain well-being and giving it to those I love... Say, I see the topic of money really interests you."

"Why do you say that?"

"Because you're asking a lot of questions about it."

"I'm just curious. I want to get to know you better, too."

"Are you serious?"

"Yeah."

"Great. But let me tell you, Arturo, money isn't everything."

"I know it isn't—there are other things also: possessions, property, stocks, investments in..."

"I'm being serious."

"I am too."

"I mean, yes, money is certainly important, but there are more valuable things—like friendship, love."

"I'm not saying those things aren't important."

"Well, it seems like the only thing that interests you is money."

"Why do you think that?"

"Because it was the first question you asked me."

"But that doesn't have anything to do with it. I asked you because it was the first thing that occurred to me. It's part of the whole picture as you say. Or are you going to say you really care that I like hamburgers? No, right?"

"All right. What else do you want to know about me?"

"How old were you when you had your first relationship?"

"Nineteen."

"Really?"

"Yes. Does it seem I got a late start?"

"No. And was it with a man?"

"Yes."

"And how old was he?"

 "You really want to know?"

"Yeah. How old was he?"

"Fifty."

"Hmm. And why's that? Did you like older men?"

"Let's just say that was how things occurred. I hadn't planned anything, nor was I thinking anything was even going to happen. It simply turned out that way. That's life—at times you don't know why things happen the way they do."

"And have you been in love many times?"

"Really in love?"

"Yeah."

"Not many."

"How many times?"

"Let me see: one...two...three, four times."

"Oh, that's not very many."

"Well, you don't always find someone who fully fits the bill, someone who gives you *everything* you need."

"And have you had many sexual experiences?"

"Think about how old I am."

"Then you've been very...?, how should I say...?"

"Promiscuous?"

"Hot to trot. Have you slept around a lot?"

"I wouldn't say it like that. I would say it more like...before...it was a different time... there was more freedom. Well, I don't know if there was more freedom, but people weren't so afraid of sex."

"Come on, it's the same thing. You slept around even though you might say it differently."

"Let me explain: I think that sex is a very important necessity—especially when you are young—it's a necessity you can't ignore. I believe if people weren't so scared, they would continue having sex like before."

"Well, that might be true for people your age because my friends aren't afraid of sex."

"How irresponsible! You're not frightened either?"

"Your turn to ask questions is over, Santiago."

"But you're careful, aren't you? You've been careful the times that...?"

"I said your turn to ask questions is over."

"Hey listen, it seems to me you're quite a little dictator."

"And you, what do you like most?"

"During sex?"

"Well, I was thinking in general, but if you want to tell me about what you like during sex, that's fine."

"I especially like to feel loved."

"Oh, that's really sweet!"

"Hey look, don't be a smart aleck, all right? Love is extremely important in a relationship with a partner."

"All right, but when it's not a relationship with a partner, what do you like?"

"At my age, sex for the sake of sex doesn't interest me."

"All right, but before...?"

"Well, I don't know, everything...I like to please the

other person. Do you know what the words 'to please' really mean?"

"To fulfill pleasures."

"It's more than that. It means to give pleasure to the other person, to find pleasure in the pleasure of the other person: to please together…to enjoy with someone—a shared pleasure."

"Ah. And what are you going to do today?"

"I don't know. Maybe I'll go out to eat. What about you—are you going out?"

"Yeah."

"Where?"

"I don't know yet. But I'm bored with being here."

"Behave yourself, all right?"

"I always behave myself."

"Really?"

"Yeah, and you?"

"Me too. At my age all I can do is to behave myself."

"Come on, get off it—you talk about your age all the time. What, do you already feel like you're ancient?"

"No, I was kidding. I'm not going to behave because of my age. I'm going to behave so you take notice."

"Why do you want me to take notice?"

"So…so you accept my friendship."

"I don't care whether or not you behave."

"Really?"

"Really."

"Well I do care if you behave."

"Ah."

"Are you going to behave?"

"I just told you I would."

"All right. When can I call you?"

"Didn't we already agree on this weekend?"

"*Not until* the weekend? Can't I call you before then?"

"Fine, then call me whenever you want. You don't have to ask for permission."

"I'm not asking for permission, Arturo. I'm simply asking when I can call you. I don't want to call at the wrong time."

"Don't worry—call me whenever you want."

"Oh, don't say that to me, because if you do, I'm going to call every hour. I really enjoy chatting with you."

"Call me whenever you want but not every hour, O.K.?"

"O.K. Have fun."

"You too. See you."

"Talk to you later, Arturo."

3

"How are you?"

"Fine. And you?"

"I'm fine too. I miss you."

"So you're not so fine."

"I guess not, huh?"

"I thought you were going to call yesterday."

"I'm sorry—did I tell you I was going to call?"

"No. I just thought you'd probably call."

"Would you have liked me to call?"

 "Maybe."

"Why?"

"I was really bored."

"Darn...I wish I had known... Well, but you could have phoned me—collect of course."

"Calling collect is really expensive."

"I wouldn't have cared. In fact, I would have liked it. Now you know for the future, all right?"

"O.K."

"Did you get what I sent you?"

"Yeah. Are they really Dutch?"

"Of course."

"They must have cost you a fortune."

"You deserve that and more. When did they arrive?"

"This morning."

"Did you like them?"

"Yeah, but you shouldn't have bothered, Santiago."

"Allow yourself some pleasure. Why is it hard for you to accept gifts?"

"It's not hard for me—it's just that I don't like flowers."

"Didn't you tell me you liked Dutch tulips?"

"Well, yeah, but I could have told you anything."

"And I wanted to give you a surprise... I'm a little slow, aren't I?"

"Why slow?"

"Oh, gullible, naïve—I didn't realize you were just pulling my leg. And at times I feel I only have one to stand on."

"I wasn't pulling your leg, Santiago—what happened was that I thought we were just having a meaningless chat; I didn't think you were really going to send me something like that."

"Would you have preferred for me to have asked you what you wanted me to send you?"

"You really want to know?"

"Yes."

"Well, yeah."

"And what would you have liked for me to send you?"

"I don't know...a CD for example."

"You like music?"

"Yeah."

"What kind of music?"

"Rock."

"Well, next time I'll send you a CD so you can forgive me for being so silly as to have sent you tulips."

"Come on, don't get carried away. It wasn't that silly. It's just that it seems to me you're a little...what's the word?"

"I don't know. What word are you trying to think of?"

"What do you call people who don't think much of themselves?"

"Insecure. Inadequate."

"No, man, it starts with a D."

"Devalued?"

"No."

"Depressive."

"No, man, what do you mean by 'depressive'?"

"Discouraged."

"I'm really not sure it starts with a D."

"What then?"

"Forget it. How long are you going to be there?"

"Three or four days. Is there something I can do for you?"

"No, I didn't ask because of that."

"But really, if you want me to get you something, I'd be happy to."

"Hmmm..."

"Think about what you want, and you can tell me later."

"O.K."

"Whatever you want, all right? Really."

"I'll think about it."

"And what were you doing?"

"Before you called?"

"Yes."

"I was just watching T.V."

"Anything special?"

"No, there wasn't anything interesting on."

"Well, I went to a really good concert yesterday."

"What group?"

"Well, it wasn't a rock group. It was a classical music concert."

"Ah. How was it?"

"It was quite good. Do you like classical music?"

"Sometimes."

"What selection do you like best? Do you have a favorite composer?"

"Hey, you're not going to send me a classical music CD, are you?"

"No, take it easy. We already agreed you would tell me what you wanted me to get you."

"It would be a waste of money."

"It seems to me you don't like that kind of music, or am I wrong?"

"Yeah, I like it—but only every now and then. Besides, I don't know much about it."

"Do you like opera?"

"Absolutely not, opera is really annoying—it's so boring."

"Fine. I promise never to invite you to the opera... Where are you right now?"

"Do you mean in what part of the house?"

"Yes."

"In the T.V. room."

"Are you sitting down?"

"I'm lying down. Why do you ask?"

"Just wondering."

"You're really curious, Santiago. You want to know everything."

"It's so I can better visualize what you're doing."

"Ah."

"And how are you dressed?"

"Shorts."

"Tight or loose, like bermudas?"

"Tight."

"You probably look really...sexy."

"You were going to say ripped, weren't you?"

"No, why do you think that?"

"Or hot."

"I was not. I respect you, Arturo."

"That wouldn't be disrespectful."

"No, I guess not. But I wasn't going to say that—really. I just couldn't think of the word I wanted."

"Ah."

"What color are your shorts?"

"Blue. With a little palm tree."

"What kind of blue?"

"Dark blue."

"Navy blue?"

"No, man—it's an electric blue. I don't know what the name of the color is."

"Indigo?"

"I don't know."

"All right. What else?"

"What else about what?"

"What else are you wearing?"

"Nothing else."

"Aren't you wearing a shirt, a T-shirt?"

"No. It's way too hot. Is it hot there?"

"Yes, it really is."

"Is it true it's going to get hotter each year?"

"That's what they say. You're not wearing shoes—not even

tennis shoes?"

"No."

"Not even underwear?"

"No."

"And that's how you're walking around the house, with those tight fitting shorts...without anything on above or below?"

"Yeah, so what?"

"Well, you probably have the servants really excited. I bet they're all walking around with their tongues hanging out just because of how you look."

"What are you talking about? Besides, there's no one here. The maids already left."

"What about the chauffeur?"

"My mother took him to Cuernavaca. There was no reason to leave him here."

"Then you're all alone?"

"Yeah."

"Poor thing. You should have invited a friend over to keep you company. No, it's better you didn't. Who knows if your friend could resist the temptation?"

"Calm down; no way that would happen!"

"If I were that friend, I wouldn't be able to control myself."

"Hey, you think all anyone thinks about is sex, don't you?"

"Of course. It's just that it's hard for some people to admit it."

"Not everyone is like you, Santiago."

"Are you saying I'm sexually obsessive?"

"More like an obese-sexual—I mean homosexual."

"Do you seriously think I'm fat?"

"No, man—I was just kidding."

"Because if you think I'm fat, I'll go on a diet."

"I just said I didn't, man. Don't take everything so seriously."

"Are you sweating?"

"No, why?"

"Just wondering since you said it was so hot."

"And you?"

"No. It hasn't rained there?"

"I haven't noticed. Hey, your voice sounds a little funny."

"What do you mean 'funny'?"

"Strange—like you're sick. Are you sick?"

"No. I mean yes—I'm lovesick. I'm obsessed with you. I haven't been able to sleep well. I wake up every night very...with a strange sensation, covered in sweat."

"It must be because of the heat."

"No, it's not because of the heat—all the houses here have air-conditioning."

"Ah."

"But seriously, Arturo, I've been going around in a daze. Ever since I met you, I'm just not the same. I don't do anything except think about you all the time. I'm beginning to worry about myself."

"Well, go see a doctor."

"Why? Do you really think I'm sick? Do you think I sound bad?"

"You're the one who's saying that."

"Well, it is a sickness, but it's a sickness the doctors can't cure. When you're lovesick, the only thing that can cure you is love."

"Ah."

"Does it bother you I'm telling you these things?"

"No, why?"

"I don't know—maybe you're not used to them."

"And how do you know I'm not used to them?"

"You're right. I'm just being foolish. Surely I'm not the first nor the only one. How naive of me!"

"I was just kidding, man. You take everything so seriously, Santiago."

"And you act like everything is a joke."

"That's just how I am. You don't like that?"

"No, no, that's not it at all, but...don't think it's easy for me to say these things, Arturo. It's really hard for me. I feel a little ridiculous all of a sudden."

"Then why do you say them?"

"Because I'm trying to make an effort to be honest with you from the beginning. I'm even willing to run the risk of you rejecting me and of you disapproving of the way I...the way I talk about things or express myself."

"I'm not rejecting you, Santiago."

"Yes, I know, but...at times I have the impression the way I'm trying to show my interest in you bothers you."

"What are you talking about?"

"That I'm interested in you...I want to date you...I'm pursuing you."

"That doesn't bother me. Why do you think it does?"

"Because you don't seem to take me very seriously."

"Well, one thing is I may not take you seriously, and another is it may bother me that you're pursuing me."

"You see how you are?"

"Why is it supposed to bother me? On the contrary..."

"Anybody would say you're not used to receiving love. I mean, if I didn't know you, if I didn't know Sarita had given you a lot of love, I would think you're reacting this way because you're not accustomed to having people love you."

"Maybe it's just the other way around. I've gotten too much love, and that's why I'm so...what am I trying to say?"

"Annoyed?"

"Overloaded, don't you think?"

"No, don't say that. I believe you can suffer due to a lack of love, but not because of an excess of love, don't you?"

"..."

"Any way, when you think I'm being annoying, tell me, all right?"

"O.K."

"So what are you going to do today?"

"Nothing."

"You're not going out?"

"I don't think so."

"Even better."

"Why?"

"That way you risk less danger."

"See how the only thing you think about is sex?"

"This time I was not thinking about sex."

"Admit it, man—why won't you admit it?"

"Seriously, I was not thinking about sex, Arturo."

"Then what were you thinking about?"

"Well, about...well, there are many kinds of dangers, like...well, I was also thinking about sex."

"You see?"

"Does it bother you?"

"No."

"It's just that you're beginning to matter too much to me, Arturo. The very idea that...that you're running around there and that you could become interested in someone else makes me crazy."

"That I could become interested in someone besides who?"

"Well, the very idea you could become interested in someone—in anyone."

"Do you think I'm interested in you?"

"I don't know. I'd give anything for you to be. I'd even beg for it like they commonly say. But you're the one who has to answer that."

"You tell me: why should I be interested in you?"

"I didn't say that."

"But you thought it, didn't you?"

"No, I didn't think it. It was more like... Maybe it was only a wish. Wishful thinking."

"Oh."

"Well, but it wouldn't be that ridiculous or would it?"

"Why?"

"Well, because I'm offering my friendship... I think I have a lot to offer you... A lot of affection, a lot of support, a lot of understanding. Does that seem like too little?"

"No."

"And I offer all that unconditionally, without expecting anything in return."

"Really?"

"Sure."

"But you're expecting me to be interested in you, aren't you?"

"No, I'm not expecting that. I only said I would like that, that it wouldn't seem that crazy to me. But I'm not putting it as a condition to...to offer you my friendship."

"That's great."

"So you don't think you could be interested in me?"

"Come on, Santiago, you already asked me that. You see

how obsessive you are?"

"And what was your answer?"

"That I didn't know. That I still don't know you very well."

"Excuse me. I'm not always like this; it's only when I'm really interested in someone… my…my obsessive character should be flattering to you."

"You think so?"

"You should take it as a kind of homage."

"O.K. That's how I'll take it."

"I'll call you tomorrow?"

"Sure, if you want to."

"Are you going to be at home?"

"I think so."

"All right, I'll track you down tomorrow."

"O.K."

"In the meantime, behave yourself. And think about me once in a while."

"You do the same, all right?"

"That's the only thing I do—think of you."

"Then I'm going to ask you not to think so much about me."

"Well, I'll try not to. Take care, all right?"

"Sure… Say, anyway, thanks for the flowers."

"You're welcome. Talk to you tomorrow, Arturo."

"Until tomorrow."

4

"How have you been behaving?"

"Fine, and you?"

"Me too. I'm just calling you for a quick chat."

"Why? You don't want to spend as much on long distance calls any more?"

"No, why would you say that? Everything I can spend on you is well worth it. The thing is that I have a lot of work—I'm feeling a little overwhelmed with everything I need to do. Well, actually, I'm trying to finish up as soon as possible. I had several matters pending...and I want to get everything taken care of before I return to Mexico City. How are you doing?"

"I don't have anything pressing."

"I'm not talking about that. How are you?"

"Fine."

"Have you thought about what you want me to bring you?"

"Yeah. Does it matter if it's a few things?"

"No, not at all, but it's best if you tell me tomorrow. That way you'll have even more time to think if you want something else. I'll make a note of it so I don't forget anything."

"I'm going to make a list, O.K.?"

"O.K. What are you plans for today?"

"I'm not sure yet."

"Has Sarita returned yet?"

"No, she said she'd get back sometime tonight."

"Tell her 'hi' for me, please."

"Do you want me to tell her you called, then?"

"No, it's better you don't tell her 'hi.' I'll call her personally to say hello. By the way, what do you think she'd like for me to bring her?"

"I don't know. You know what she likes better than I do."

"Some perfume?"

"Maybe."

"What kind of perfume?"

"Oh, I don't know. Maybe you should just buy her some tea."

"What do you mean? There isn't any tea there?"

"Well, I don't know, but that's always what she's asking for."

"All right, then, that's what I'll bring her. You gave me a good idea... And how are you going to behave?"

"Fine, man—I already told you."

"No, you didn't tell me you were going to behave well. You said you had behaved well."

"You must think I'm really slutty, don't you?"

"Hey, come on, what kind of language is that?"

"Do you really think I am?"

"No, no, not at all, Arturo."

"Then how come you're always so concerned about how I have behaved and how I'm going to behave?"

"Well,...it's surely because I'm very insecure. Forgive me."

"..."

"Do you forgive me?"

"Yeah, man, but don't be so insistent."

"It must be because I have so much work, don't you think?"

"And what does that have to do with anything?"

"Well, it's just that when you're overworked, you get tense and...and you end up nagging everybody."

"Oh."

"But now that I'm finishing up, I'm going to be a new person—you won't even recognize me."

"O.K."

"Well, I'm going to get back to work."

"Remember time is money."

"Send me a kiss so I can clear my mind and concentrate on my work."

"Uh-huh."

"So tell me."

"I send you a kiss."

"Thanks. And I send one to you. I'll call you tomorrow."

"Sure."

"Talk to you tomorrow, Arturo. Have a good one."

"Ciao."

5

"Did you write everything down?"

"Yes. This afternoon I'll go buy everything. Are you sure you don't want anything else?"

"I'm sure."

"Did your mother get back?"

"Yeah."

"And how did everything go?"

"Fine. I guess fine. I haven't talked to her."

"Is she at home right now?"

"Yeah."

"What's she doing?"

"Nothing. She's on the phone also. You want me to put her on?"

"No. I'd better talk to her later."

"So when are you coming back?"

"Tomorrow."

"Have you already made your reservation?"

"Yes, of course...Say, Arturo, now that I'm returning, I'd like to take you out to dinner."

"Where?"

"Wherever you'd like. Do you accept my invitation?"

"When?"

"The day after tomorrow."

"I can't—I already have something to do."

"With whom?"

"With some friends."

"And you can't change your plans with them?"

"Oh no, impossible. It would be better to invite me another day."

"I'll invite you whenever you'd like, but couldn't we at least see each other for a little while on Wednesday...even if it's just for a cup of coffee?"

"We'll see."

"That way I can give you what I bought you."

"O.K., but just for a while."

"And when can we have dinner?"

"Would Friday be all right?"

"Not until Friday? I'll die of impatience."

"Don't exaggerate, man."

"Can't we get together on Thursday?"

"..."

"Well, if there's no way, I guess I'll just have to wait until Friday."

"Write it down in your appointment book."

"What makes you think I'll forget? You're the one who should write it down."

"I won't forget either."

"Why? Because you're interested in seeing me?"

"Because you're going to be in charge of reminding me all the time."

"Hey, hold on...you're implying that I'm nagging."

"No, man, what makes you think that? I was joking."

"I really like how you are, Arturo—you're so playful in the way you change your mind so quickly. You always have a clever answer for everything. Don't ever change."

"O.K."

"Although if I were to be completely honest, your joking around sometimes makes me feel insecure."

"Why?"

"Well, because...I'm often the target of your jokes, and... Suddenly, I get the impression you're making fun of me."

"Why do you say that? You're the one who's saying I'm only joking. Let's see...what does 'joke' mean?"

"It means...well, it's something you don't say seriously—but rather when you're playing around."

"There you have it. Then you're the one who's wrong because you're the one who's taking it seriously."

"Yes, you're right...No, it's just that I've had some hard knocks in life and...well, and it makes a person a little resentful, hurt. I don't know...At times it makes a person distrustful."

"You don't trust me?"

"No, no, I'm not saying that, Arturo. What I'm trying to say is ...when you've been hurt, you're afraid you're going to get hurt again."

"What, you don't know how to protect yourself?"

"What happens is that it's difficult to believe again. And I want to believe in you, Arturo. Give me the opportunity to believe again."

"All right. Is it really true you've been hurt many times?"

"Yes, well, maybe not many times, but at my age it's difficult to deal with failure—especially when it comes to love. When you get to a certain age, the only thing you want is a peaceful life without surprises."

"Do you think that's why my mother doesn't fuck anymore? So she doesn't have to put herself at risk?"

"Maybe...But how do you know Sarita doesn't...she doesn't have sex any more?"

"Well, you can just tell, can't you? Or maybe she still does fuck?"

"I don't know. We haven't spoken about those things."

"Aren't you guys good friends?"

"Well, yes, we're very good friends, but... Look, your mother and I have a very special relation, very...how should I describe it? Very spiritual. We almost never talk about that."

"Then what do you talk about?"

"About many other things...about what happens to us, about..."

"Sex is something that happens, isn't it?"

"Yes, of course, you're completely right, but at our age it's not such an important priority. Like I told you the other day—a person thinks about meaningful things, more in line with what's going on at that moment in time."

"Maybe you don't think my mother should look for a boyfriend?"

"I don't know. Perhaps she doesn't need one."

"She's still attractive...she's got a nice figure."

"Would you like for your mother to have a boyfriend?"

"Yeah."

"How come?"

"Because that way she would have someone to entertain her, and she would be less neurotic. You're not going to tell her anything about this conversation, are you?"

"I won't—why would you even ask that? In the same way I trust you, I'd like for you to trust me. All right?"

"O.K."

"Why do you say Sarita is neurotic?"

"Come on Santiago, you know her quite well—don't be so naive. You don't think she's neurotic?"

"Well, I wouldn't say it like that. I'd say Sarita is a very special person; she's not like common folk. She has...she has her idiosyncrasies, of course. She's a very strong woman, very intelligent, very direct. Maybe even a little abrupt every now and then, but she also has a great sense of humor; she's very dynamic, and...and she knows how to be generous. I find her absolutely fascinating—in all the years I have known her, I have never gotten bored of her."

"I didn't say she was boring. I said she was neurotic."

"Besides, the poor thing has suffered a lot. Life's hard knocks also leave a mark on you; they harden you. Maybe that's why she's a little...abrupt, like I was saying."

"It doesn't seem to me she has suffered so much."

"Hey, don't say that. What do you know?"

"I really think you have the wrong idea about her."

"Why?"

"Maybe you're talking to me about how my mother was before. But now I see everything is going very well for her—she has a lot of friends, she goes out a lot, she has a good time."

"Well, it's that she's an intelligent person—she lives intelligently; she tries to put a positive spin on things, but that doesn't mean she hasn't suffered."

"You guys stopped seeing each other for a long time, didn't you?"

"Something like thirteen years."

"Why? Did you have a fight?"

"No, no."

"Did you get into a fight over a man?"

"Not at all, no way; don't say that—that's silly. What happened was ...our lives simply took different paths. I was spending a lot of time living elsewhere... Well, in all friendships there are periods when you feel especially close—with a lot of intimacy...and there are other periods of...how should I put it?...of lapses. There can be a separation without an end to caring and affection, don't you think?"

"It could be. But then, if you separate yourself from your friends, you can't see how they're changing. Maybe in the thirteen years you stopped seeing my mother, she became neurotic, don't you think?"

"Well, you believe whatever you'd like."

"But it is possible, right?"

"You always want to be right, Arturo. And that's not good. Do you want me to agree with you even though I'm not convinced that she is?"

"If you're not convinced about what I'm telling you, it's because you're not a good observer."

"Then why do you think your mother is neurotic?"

"Come on, man—all you have to do is to look at her. She's very...what do you call someone who always wants to get their way?"

"Willful."

"No, man...domineering. She's very domineering—you always have to do things the way she wants. If you don't, she goes nuts."

"All right, yes, you're somewhat right about that."

"She's also very demanding, isn't she? She always demands too much. She demands too much attention. She always wants everyone to cater to her every whim. She always has to be the center of attention."

"Well, if she demands a lot it's because she also gives a lot."

"Are we going to continue talking about her for the whole time? I'm already bored."

"You're the one who brought her up."

"Me? Well, let's change topics. Where were we before we started talking about her?"

"We...I don't remember. But we can get back to my favorite topic: 'you'."

"I'm your favorite topic?"

"Yes."

"In all of your conversations?"

"Yes. Well, in all of my thoughts. I haven't spoken to anyone about you yet."

"That's just as well."

"Why? Would it bother you if your name were always on the tip of my tongue?"

"Oh, how funny you are, Santiago, really."

"Why do you think it's better I not talk about you?"

"Never mind."

"Are you afraid your mother is going to find out?"

"If she found out, the only one who'd stand to lose would be you."

"You think so?"

"Sure."

"Well then, it's better she doesn't find out. I don't want to lose what matters to me most right now."

"You should have said, 'At this moment and always'."

"At this moment and always."

"Amen."

"Seriously, you are the only thing that matters to me, Arturo."

"I'm really that important to you? Would you be willing to give up everything for me?"

"May I make an observation?"

"Go ahead."

"At times you also speak like they do in soap operas."

"Maybe, but the difference is you're so serious, and I'm

only joking. What's worse is you don't even realize it."

"You always outwit me when we talk... You're too intelligent, Arturo. Listen carefully to what I'm telling you: too intelligent."

"And what's wrong with that?"

"It's no good. People who are too intelligent suffer a lot."

"Why?"

"Because not everyone is like them. They get so exasperated. They become intolerant. They end up not being able to handle people."

"Like my mother."

"Do you see who's the one bringing up the topic?"

"But weren't you also thinking about her when you said that?"

"Well, yes—that's true: Sarita suffers a lot because of that. And that's precisely why she has serious problems relating to other people—she can't stand stupidity; she can't tolerate the slightest weakness; she can't stand the flaws all human beings have. As you see, she even has problems with the servants."

"And do you think I'm like her?"

"No, I didn't say that. But I do think you should be a little bit more...understanding."

"I promise I'll try."

"You're making fun of me again."

"Seriously, I'm not, Santiago."

"The tone you used led me to believe you were."

"Well, you're wrong. Let me tell you you're wrong."

"All right, all right—let's talk about something else. Tell me how you're dressed. Are you in shorts?"

"No."

"Then in what?"

"Guess."

"Some jeans?"

"Yeah."

"Denim?"

"No."

"Corduroy?"

"Come on, Santiago, corduroy in this heat?"

"Well then, cotton?"

"Uh-huh."

"And they're...blue?"

"Yeah."

"What shade of blue? Light blue?"

"Yeah."

"And you're also wearing a shirt...is it light colored also?"

"No."

"But it's just one color?"

"No."

"Striped?"

"No."

"It has several colors. A Hawaiian shirt?"

"More or less."

"I bet you look really handsome."

"Normal. Like always."

"Which is to say *very* handsome."

"Don't believe it. There are days when I look awful."

"Don't say that, Arturo...at your age people always look good."

"When I don't bathe for example."

"I don't believe it."

"You will one day."

"I like it when you talk like that, Arturo."

"Like how?"

"I liked it when you said I'd believe it one day."

"Why?"

"Because that means we're going to continue to see each other."

"Well, sure...didn't you say you wanted us to become friends?"

"Yes, certainly...that's what I want most."

"Well then, we'll be friends."

"Just friends?"

"Oh, Santiago."

"All right; I won't be a nuisance about that...I promise."

"O.K."

"I'll let you rest now."

"O.K."

"But we're going to at least see each other on Wednesday, right?"

"Yeah, we already said for a little while, didn't we?"

"I'll call you tomorrow so we can make definite plans."

"Oh, I think it would be better if we make the plans now."

"Why? Would it bother you if I called you tomorrow?"

"No, but I'm not going to be home tomorrow."

"Are you going out?"

"Santiago, if I'm telling you I'm not going to be home, it's because I'm going out, right?"

"All right. Where do you want to meet?"

"Where would you like to?"

"You want me to come by and get you?"

"No. I have to go out to dinner later—I already told you

that."

"I can take you."

"I'm going in the car."

"And you couldn't ask me to accompany you to the dinner?"

"No."

"Well, where is this famous dinner?"

"In the Lomas neighborhood[3]."

"Then we could see each other in... What do you think if we met in the Zona Rosa[4]?"

"Oh, it would be better if we met up at the Sanborns[5] in Chapultepec[6]."

"The one in front of the movie theater?"

"Is there any other one?"

"No, right? What time do you want to meet?"

"At eight."

"Good, then it's set. You really don't want me to call to remind you?"

"No."

"All right. See you Wednesday."

"O.K."

"Aren't you going to wish me bon voyage?"

"Bon voyage, Santiago."

"Thanks, Arturo. I'm dying to see you."

"Well, hold on a little bit—don't die before we get to see each other."

"Your wish is my command. See you Wednesday, Arturo."

"Ciao."

6

"Yeah, man—you told me just a little while ago."

"But I'm going to say it again: I really enjoy seeing you, Arturo. You don't know how much I like it."

"Me too."

"Are you serious?"

"No."

"You see what you're like? And wouldn't it be possible for you...for you to not go to your dinner?"

"..."

"Don't make that face. It's just that I'd like to be with you a little longer. I enjoy your company so much."

"Well, you'll have to enjoy it another day because I really have to go."

"Right now? But you just got here."

"We said we were only going to see each other for a little while, right? And you agreed."

"Well, yes, but..."

"We've already been here for an hour."

"Well, but... What's wrong? I'm not really what you were expecting? Does my being here upset you?"

"No, why?"

"I don't know. It's not the same talking to someone on the phone as it is face to face. Maybe you had another impression of me, and you feel deceived now that you see me in person."

"Oh come on—don't say such silly things."

"After all, it's only the second time we've seen each other."

"That's not true. When I was a boy, I saw you many times."

"Well, yes, but it's not the same—both of us have changed a lot since then."

"That's for sure."

"Maybe you think I look too old...or...I don't know. Be honest—are you sure my presence doesn't bother you?"

"No, man."

"Then why do you want to leave?"

"I already told you: I have plans."

"You're making me feel insecure."

"Well there you go—the one doesn't have anything to do with the other."

"Then let me stay a little while longer with you."

"I can't. I have to go."

"Let me go with you."

"Come on, Santiago, I already told you no."

"No, I'm not saying for you to invite me to your dinner. I'm asking you to let me accompany you to the door."

"And are you going to leave the car here?"

"Yes."

"And how are you going to get back?"

"Don't you worry. That's my problem. I can take a taxi. Come on, let me go with you."

"Well, if you want..."

"Let's go then."

"You're not going to wait for the change?"

"No. Let's just leave it as the tip, all right?"

"That's a lot of money, Santiago."

"Well, then I hope she considers it a gift. Just as life is rewarding me with this opportunity to see you, so the waitress is getting an unexpected gift. You have to be generous when you get something. If you're not, it's bad karma."

"Really?"

"Yes. I'm firmly convinced."

"And what are you going to do today?"

"I don't know. I think I'm going to rest."

"It's still really early, man. You should go out to dinner or to a bar."

"Last night I didn't sleep well—again."

"Why not?"

"You already know. I already told you."

"Because of me?"

"Yes."

"You're really...as you said, very obsessed with me?"

"Let's not speak in Spanish right now. Someone may hear us[7]."

"So what? Maybe you're embarrassed about the way you feel?"

"Of course not. It's just that I don't want to share this feeling with others[8]."

"O.K., O.K."

"I couldn't sleep again. I was thinking about you all night long. I was very...very upset. I'm getting a little scared."

"You shouldn't."

"Why? Because you're going to help me?"

"Because it's not good for your health. You're going to get old soon."

"*Older*, you mean. Look at me, I'm turning gray."

"Did you say 'gay?' You've always been gay; man, don't fool yourself."

"Come on. Where did you park the car?"

"Right here, at the door...⁹ Come on, Santiago, you're really sort of comical—do you really think if we speak in English people won't find out?"

"Comical or naive?"

"Both."

"Do you want me to drive?"

"No, I'll drive. Are you serious about wanting to accompany me?"

"Of course. I already told you I was."

"O.K."

"When are you ever going to give in and say 'yes' to me?"

"Do you want me to give in and say 'yes' to you, or do you want me to give you something else?"

"All of the above."

"Because if what you want is for me to give you my ass, it's not going to be so easy."

"Hey, hey, what...what kind of language is that?"

"What's the problem? It's what you really want, isn't it?"

"Well, yes, but there are ways of saying things like that without being so vulgar."

"It's just the same."

"All right; maybe you're right, but...would it be a big deal for you to give it to me?"

"It would be a *very* costly deal for you. My cheeks are worth their weight in gold."

"Hey, I don't know what to think."

"Come on—I'm joking, man. You take everything so seriously."

"No, that's not true, not everything. I have a good sense

of humor also. I brag about it. It's that I really take *you* seriously."

"Get off of it. You don't have to take anything seriously. That's why you're getting so many gray hairs."

"Yes, really? Do you think I look bad?"

"No."

"Do you think it would be a good idea for me to dye my hair?"

"Yeah."

"Are you serious?"

"Sure, how about Mexican pink?"

"See how you are, Arturo?"

"'See how you are, Santiago'."

"Listen to me, don't talk to me in that mocking tone."

"I'm telling you that you don't look bad the way you are, and you ask me if you should dye your hair: 'listen to me'."

"Please forgive me."

"Where is that expression 'Listen to me' from? Guadalajara?"

"Maybe. Then you think I'm O.K. the way I look?"

"Yeah, man. I already told you."

"Your wish is my command. We won't talk about it any more."

"Fine."

"Then you forgive me?"

"For what?"

"My nagging, my insecurities."

"I forgive your nagging, but don't be so insistent any more."

"It must be hard to put up with me..."

"A little."

"Humor me. Keep in mind I'm a poor old man in love."

"Get off it."

"Crazy to be with you, crazy over desire... When old guys like me fall in love, we become ridiculous... Look at the hold you have on me—I can't sleep, I'm out of sorts... I don't know what's going to happen to me. Look how my heart pounds just being with you... Feel it."

"You're sure it's not the altitude or the pollution that's affecting you?"

"No, Arturo. It's being with you that gets me this way. You don't know...the only thing I do is to think about you all the time."

"You're so obsessive!"

"I'm always dying to be with you."

"You're with me right now, aren't you?"

"No, I'm not talking about... I want to be with you alone."

"Well, we're alone now unless there's somebody else in the car."

"You know what I'm talking about, Arturo."

"Are you talking about fucking?"

"Well, I wouldn't say it like that; I'd..."

"I know you wouldn't say it like that, but that's what you're talking about, isn't it?"

"Wow, you're incredibly direct."

"But that's what you want, isn't it? To fuck me?"

"Yes, that's what I want. But I want to make love to you. I want to caress you, I want to talk to you, to take care of you; I want...to love you and everything else that implies. I want to give you everything, Arturo. Sex is just a part of it."

"..."

"Does it frighten you I'm telling you these things?"

"No, it doesn't frighten me, but it seems to me what you're asking is a lot."

"Yes, it's a lot. What I'm asking is everything. But I'm also willing to give everything."

"Can I turn up the radio a little?"

"If you want, but don't try to change the subject."

"What do you mean? You want me to answer you right now?"

"No, no, not at all. I don't want to pressure you. I want you to think about it carefully...consider what I'm offering you—weigh the pros and cons, the advantages and disadvantages. Later you can give me an answer, but don't take too long. Don't make me suffer too much."

"All right."

"You'll think about it?"

"Yeah."

"..."

"..."

"I feel like doing something really crazy."

"Like naming me as your universal heir. That would be awesome!"

"Come on, now you're giving me something to think about... No it's not that."

"Then what do you feel like doing?"

"Giving you a kiss right this minute."

"Come on, there's nothing crazy about that."

"For me there is. Would you let me?"

"O.K., give me one."

"I can?"

"Yeah, I just said you could."

"...Hmmm, that was really nice."

"Hey, be careful, man—you're going to distract me. I thought you were going to kiss me on the cheek."

"Can I give you another one?"

"No, you only said one."

"But I really want to give you another one."

"Uh, that way we'll never finish—after this one, you'll want to give me another one, and then another."

"And what would be wrong with that?"

"Wrong?...nothing, but we're almost there. You're going to be 'out of sorts' as you like to say."

"Just one more, all right?"

"O.K."

"... Oh, Arturo, you drive me crazy..."

"You said one more and that would be it."

"Well, yes, I only gave you one."

"Take your hand off of me then."

"Does that bother you?"

"That's enough, Santiago, I'm asking you to take your hand off of me."

"Don't be afraid—I'm not going to..."

"I'm not afraid—I just don't want you to touch me right now."

"Why not?"

"Because I don't. Leave me alone, O.K.?"

"All right. I'm going to do it just so you can see how much I respect you, how I respect your wishes, even though they go against what I want."

"O.K."

"Forgive my presumptuousness."

"It's all right."

"It's just that I can't control myself. You don't know what this is like..."

"Yeah, I do. You already told me, and I understood."

"Be more tolerant with me, Arturo. Put yourself in my place."

"Should I let you out here? It's probably easier to catch a taxi here."

"You're right."

"There you go."

"Can I call you tomorrow?"

"If you want to."

"Of course I want to. I always want to talk to you."

"O.K., then call me."

"Take care then."

"You too."

"I'll take care, but it will be because of you, because you asked me to."

"O.K."

"See you later. Thanks."

"See you."

"Talk to you tomorrow, Arturo."

"Ciao...say, thanks for the things you bought me."

"You're welcome. I'm glad you liked them."

"I didn't say that I liked them; I only said thanks."

"All right, Arturo. You're welcome."

"But I did like them, all right?"

"Take care."

7

"So how did your dinner go?"

"Fine."

"Did you have fun?"

"Yeah."

"How late did you stay?"

"I don't know."

"What time did you get home?"

"I said I don't know. I wasn't paying attention, but I got home early."

"And today...how was your day?"

"Fine also."

"What did you do?"

"Come on, Santiago, you're sure asking a lot of questions. I think it would be better for you to tell me how your day was."

"Very well. Good, more or less. I found some problems with the house; I have to make some repairs; I had to call the plumber—you know—the typical stuff when you're away for a while...nothing out of the ordinary. Just a bunch of tedious things you just have to deal with."

"Oh."

"And you...what did you do?"

"I didn't do anything interesting either."

"But you did go out, didn't you?"

"Yeah, why?"

"Because I called you several times and couldn't get a hold of you."

"Well, you got a hold of me now."

"And what are you going to do? Are you going to go out again?"

"No. I had plans, but I think I'm just going to go to bed. I'm really out of it."

"What do you mean you're really out of it? Didn't you get back early from your dinner?"

"I did, but I stayed up really late watching television."

"You shouldn't watch so much television."

"Why not?"

"You're at your prime as a young man...you should take advantage of your time to do other things."

"Like see you?"

"That's not a bad idea. When are we going to get together?"

"Didn't we already agree on tomorrow? You're getting insistent again."

"No, I was just testing you to see if you remembered... Boy, I really want to be with you, Arturo... What are you wearing right now?"

"Just some pants."

"What color?"

"Blue."

"You really like blue, don't you?"

"Yeah."

"You wore a blue shirt yesterday, and when I called you the other day, you told me you were wearing blue shorts."

"You notice everything."

"Because everything matters to me when it has to do with you... Did you know blue is a very cold color?"

"What do you mean 'cold'?"

"Yes, cold. There are warm colors and cold colors."

"Well, it's really hot outside: it should be all right then for me to put on a cold color, shouldn't it?"

"Could be, but cold colors keep you from communicating with others, while the warmer colors encourage it."

"Really?"

"Sure. If you don't believe me, pay attention the next time you're at a get-together. If you wear a warm color, it's more likely people will constantly come up to you to chat."

"Oh."

"Although, like with all rules, there are surely exceptions—especially if it has to do with a boy as handsome as you. The good-looking ones are always the exception in everything... Surely you always get people's attention, and people are always coming up to you to chat..."

"More or less."

"What else are you wearing?"

"A T-shirt."

"I bet you look really handsome, very sexy."

"There's something to what you're saying."

"What time are we going to see each other tomorrow?"

"At eight?"

"Sure. Do you want me to come by for you?"

"No, just tell me where we're going to meet."

"Is it all right if you just come over to my house?"

"O.K., but we'll go out right away, won't we?"

"Why? What are you afraid of?"

"That you'll become really insistent."

"Are you really frightened?"

"More than being frightened—it makes me feel tired and

bored."

"Why?"

"Stop asking me so many questions."

"Just tell me why you feel tired and bored when I get insistent."

"Because I do."

"But tell me why..."

"I'm going to go to bed, all right? See you tomorrow."

"Don't hang up on me yet."

"I told you—I'm going to bed."

"But don't hang up on me quite yet. Let me be with you a little while longer...until you fall asleep."

"O.K., but just for a little while, all right?"

"You do what you have to do."

"Uh-huh."

"Where are you right now?"

"In the bedroom."

"Good, then go to bed. Just tell me what you're doing so I can feel close to you."

"O.K. Right now I'm pulling back the cover on the bed... Done... And now I'm taking off my clothes."

"What are you taking off?"

"My pants."

"Are you wearing anything else? Any underwear?"

"Yeah, briefs."

"What color are they?"

"White."

"Are you standing up?"

"Yeah."

"Tell me what you see."

"What do you mean tell you what I see?"

"Yes, tell me what you see while you're standing up. What part of your body do you see?"

"I see a part of my stomach. Then...then I see my briefs, my legs, my feet."

"Do you have a lot of hair on your legs?"

"Hardly any."

"You probably have great looking legs: firm, muscular, smooth... Do you have any chest hair?"

"No."

"I really like smooth bodies with soft skin, the kind your hand can caress without... without anything getting in the way of the caress... I don't know why I imagined you without much body hair... I really find you attractive, Arturo... Man, I'd really like to be able to see you right this minute!"

"I'm taking off my T-shirt now."

"Hmmm...that's hot."

"And now I'm going to take off my briefs."

"Are you going to sleep nude?"

"I always sleep nude."

"And what if somebody walks in on you?"

"Come on, Santiago; who's going to walk in on me?"

"I don't know: your mother, one of the servants—I don't know."

"They're supposed to knock before they enter, aren't they?"

"Yes, you're right...but tell me what you see."

"My dick and my balls."

"Wow, great. That sounds delicious. Tell me what your penis is like."

"Oh come on, I'm sure not going to tell you anything about that. You're really kind of strange, Santiago."

"Why strange?"

"Because you are, because you're strange: what crazy questions."

"Well, then you see your penis... Is it sleeping?"

"What do you mean 'sleeping'?"

"Without an erection."

"It's beginning to get hard."

"How come? Do you get turned on by seeing your own body?"

"More or less."

"Or does what I'm saying to you turn you on...talking about these things?"

"That too."

"Touch it."

"What for?"

"So you can imagine I'm the one touching it."

"Oh, Santiago."

"Touch it, Arturo."

"O.K., I'm touching it now."

"And how are you feeling?"

"I feel great...it's getting even harder."

"Grab your penis. Squeeze it a little with your hand."

"Done."

"Are you even more turned on?"

"Yeah."

"What do you feel when you touch your penis? Describe how you're feeling to me."

"It's hot...hard...I feel wonderful...I feel like jacking off."

"Don't stop on my behalf."

"What are you doing?"

"I'm stroking myself."

"Are you hard?"

"Yes, very hard...like when I was an adolescent."

"Why?"

"I get really turned on thinking about you...talking to you... Stroke yourself."

"O.K."

"But tell me how you're doing it, how you're feeling."

"...I'm squeezing my cock. I'm jacking. I'm raising and lowering the little bit of skin. What's it called?"

"Foreskin."

"I'm raising and lowering the foreskin."

"Does it feel good?"

"Yeah."

"Are you feeling really good?"

"Yeah... I'm squeezing even harder now."

"How are you? Are you standing up?"

"No, I'm sitting in bed."

"Do you feel the contact of the sheets with your butt cheeks?"

"Yeah."

"And how do you feel?"

"I feel really turned-on, too."

"Are you legs spread apart or together?"

"Spread apart."

"Caress you testicles a little with your hand."

"You too."

"Yes, me too."

"I'm going to drop the telephone."

"Hold it another way—put it between your shoulder and ear."

"O.K."

"Now, keep on caressing your testicles."

"They're called 'balls'."

"All right, keep on caressing your balls... How do they feel?"

"Hard. They're getting really hard. They're shrinking."

"That's because you're about to come. Do you want to come now?"

"Yeah."

"Then come, my love...come."

"..."

"Tell me when you come."

"Oh, I'm coming..."

"How hot! Come... Come... Shoot it all out."

"..."

"Did you come?"

"...Yeah. You?"

"No. Tell me where your semen landed."

"On the rug."

"Nowhere else?"

"Well, I got some on my hand and on my cock."

"I'm sure your semen is very potent."

"I'm going to go clean off, all right?"

"No, no, wait just a little longer."

"Are you about to come?"

"No."

"You're not turned-on?"

"Yes, but I don't want to come."

"Why not?"

"Because...because I prefer to wait for another time."

"When you fuck me?"

"Yes."

"I thought you were hesitant about that?"

"I am, why?"

"It's just a little strange. You're so sure we're going to fuck... Hold on a minute, all right?"

"Sure..."

"...I'm back."

"Listen, I'm not sure we're going to...to make love. It's my greatest desire—I'd really like to, but to be certain about that...no, no way. I never feel sure about anything, much less about something so...so important to me. So, how do you see things?"

"I don't know."

"But do I have reason to...? Should I be hopeful?"

"I don't know. You told me to think about it, didn't you?"

"Yes, but I also asked you not to make me wait too long. You don't know what you mean to me. You don't know what this wait is like."

"O.K. then. Now I'm really going to go to bed, all right?"

"Yes, Arturo. Thanks for your company. I won't bother you any more."

"All right."

"See you tomorrow then. Sleep well."

"Uh-huh."

"Dream about me."

"See you tomorrow."

"Tomorrow it is, Arturo."

8

"Sarita told me you haven't been going to school."

"Did you see her?"

"I spoke with her."

"When?"

"This morning."

"And what did she tell you?"

"Just that—you weren't going to school. She's very worried."

"Well, she's an idiot."

"Don't talk that way about your mother."

"She just doesn't understand. Of course she prefers I go to school even though I don't like anything about it."

"Well, she does it for your own good. She's thinking of what's best for you."

"Or rather what's best for her."

"No, Arturo—don't say that."

"Did she tell you to talk to me?"

"No, how can you ask that? She didn't even know we were going to see each other."

"I told her we were."

"Oh, Arturo, how insensitive! What were you thinking?"

"What's wrong with me mentioning it?"

"There's nothing wrong, but...I don't know; it just seems like an indiscretion on your part."

"Well, there's nothing I can do about it now. I already

told her."

"Oh, Arturo, see how you're acting?"

"It's not true, man. I'm just joking."

"Listen, what a ... You gave me quite a scare."

"Ha ha ha."

"You're really very intelligent, Arturo...too intelligent, like I told you the other day. Whenever the topic of conversation becomes a little uncomfortable for you—who knows how you do it—but you change the topic."

"Are you saying that because of the school thing?"

"Yes."

"You're the one supporting my position: if I'm so intelligent, there's no reason for me to go to school."

"You see? There isn't any argument you can't turn around in your favor."

"That's why you like me, right?"

"Yes, exactly, but lower your voice a little."

"You're not going to start speaking in English again, are you? Even the waiters here probably speak English."

"You're right...like always. What are you going to order?"

"I don't know. I'm still not hungry. Why don't we get another drink?"

"That seems like a very good idea. Let's toast this get-together..."

"Arturo, leave that alone please."

"It's just that it's a lot of money for a tip. You were too generous. I need the money more."

"I said to leave it alone."

"You're going to cause the waiters to get into the bad habit of expecting big tips, man. Or what, are you doing it to impress me?"

"No, I'm not doing it for that."

"Then...?"

"Well, because... I don't know—I've always been generous with the people who serve me. It seems it's the least I can do—if they treat me well, it's only right for me to do the same for them... Hurry up, put it back. Don't embarrass me."

"Oh, you... There you go. But you're going to be poor, don't you think?"

"Don't worry...that's a long way off."

"Then how will you support me?"

"Say, how very interesting. Don't tell me you're going to go out with me because of my money."

"I'm not saying I'm going to go out with you."

"Well, if you did, would it be because of my money?"

"Yeah, and what's wrong with that?"

"Listen, it's just that..."

"Didn't you tell me two days ago that...? What did you say, huh? That I should consider the pros and the cons, right?"

"Then my only virtue is my money?"

"I didn't say it was your only virtue, did I?"

"But it's the most important."

"*One* of the most important."

"And what are my other virtues?"

"Oh, Santiago, you know what they are. Don't play dumb."

"So tell me."

"What for?"

"So that... I'd like to hear something nice from you."

"Don't be...what's the word?"

"Narcissistic."

"Vain. Don't be vain. So no one has ever told you about your virtues?"

"Yes, but..."

"There you go. Then why do you want me to repeat to you what you already know?"

"Well, uh...so I can feel more secure."

"But I don't want you to feel more secure. Just think, with you always being so insistent, what would you be like if I really wound you up?"

"Well, tell me—even if it's just one thing you like about me."

"I already told you."

"Besides that."

"You told me to tell you just one, didn't you? I already told you. Don't be a drag."

"Well, but are there several?"

"Uh-huh."

"Really? More than my defects?"

"The thing is I still don't know what your defects are. I'll have to ask my mother."

"Don't get your mother involved in this. We're talking man to man. Why do you want to involve her?"

"You're the one who brought her up."

"Me?"

"Yeah, you—just a little while ago with the thing about school."

"All right, then I'm now suggesting we talk about something else."

"O.K. What do you want to talk about?"

"You. You know you're my favorite topic."

"Oh, come on—how boring."

"Seriously, Arturo, I wanted to tell you if you have

problems, let me know, but don't do these kind of things to me."

"What things?"

"You know what I'm talking about."

"Well, yeah, I do have problems. I don't have enough money."

"Sarita doesn't give you any?"

"Very little—since I quit school, she hardly gives me anything. She's getting to be really stingy. Well, she's always been stingy—you know how she is."

"I wouldn't say Sarita is stingy."

"No?"

"I'd say she has foresight; she takes care of her money."

"That's being stingy, isn't it?"

"No. A stingy person is someone who has money but who doesn't spend it on what's necessary; they deprive themselves of things just for the sake of not spending their money. Sarita has a comfortable lifestyle."

"That's what you think because that's what she wants everyone to think—but that's not the case—she suddenly has some things... Tell me she's not stingy: she locks the pantry so the maids don't drink the Cokes."

"Well, I'm sure she has her reasons. Don't judge her, Arturo. I'm sure your father's death made her feel very vulnerable."

"Maybe, but that happened a long time ago. And besides, she works and makes a good salary."

"Well, yes, but she also has a lot of expenses... Don't kid yourself—it's not easy for a single woman to bear all the responsibility for maintaining a household, especially if she's accustomed to a certain lifestyle."

"Look, that's another problem—her lifestyle as you call it. If she didn't have so many idiotic expenses that only serve to try to impress everyone else, she would have a higher standard of living, wouldn't she? She'd have more money at her disposal. Let's see, why does she need to pay a chauffeur? Doesn't that seem like a useless luxury to you?"

"No, no, not at all."

"Especially if she feels so vulnerable as you say."

"Well, but that's another thing. It's more of a question of dignity."

"What do you mean 'dignity'?"

"Of course. Look, it's a little bit like what happens in those French families who refuse to move when they suffer an economic crisis. You'd say they could easily relocate to another less elegant neighborhood and live more comfortably."

"Exactly."

"But they prefer to suck it up as they say crudely and maintain their lifestyle, their status. It's a little bit like not letting someone bend your arm all the way back when you're faced with adversity. It seems very reasonable. I certainly understand it. And I understand Sarita although it's not the same thing of course. But there are things that once you're accustomed to them, you can't give them up."

"And we keep talking about her."

"You're right, but, well, before we change the subject, I want to tell you something, and I hope you don't forget it: if you have problems of *any* type whatsoever, don't hesitate to let me know."

"O.K."

"I'm happy to do anything at all for you."

"Fine."

"Just so you know, all right? Whatever you may need, tell me: money...there's no reason why not having money should keep you from being happy."

"O.K."

"Let's go if you want. You seem a little bored."

"We can have another drink at my house, Arturo. Would you like to?"

"I don't know...you'd better take me home. It's already late, isn't it?"

"No, it's not late... I'm sure that's not the real reason why you don't want to come over."

"Then what is it?"

"Isn't it that you're afraid?"

"Of what? Of you?"

"Of being alone with me in my space."

"What are you talking about?"

"Then let's go. Besides, I have a surprise for you."

"Another one? You're going to spoil me."

"No, what I gave you wasn't a surprise; they were things you had asked me for."

"That's true."

"All right then—let's go. Don't be afraid."

"O.K."

"Oh, Santiago, why did you spend your money on this, man?"

"You don't like it?"

"Yeah, it's really cool, but I already have one."

"It doesn't matter. This brand is better. You can sell the one you already have."

"Yeah, that's true. Listen, thanks a lot. It's really cool."

"Sure; every time you use it, it will remind you of me."

"Then I'll be reminded of you all the time."

"That's better than better... Give me a kiss."

"Oh, Santiago... O.K."

"...Hmmm, you kiss really well. I was in heaven... Why are you nervous?"

"I'm not nervous. You said we were going to have another drink, didn't you?"

"Yes, of course. What would you like to drink?"

"The same as you."

"Whiskey?"

"No, not whiskey—I don't really like whiskey. I'd prefer something else."

"I'm going to fix you something really delicious."

"O.K."

"Why don't you put on some music?"

"Like what?"

"Well, go look and see what you might like. I'm sure you'll find something. Do you like sweet drinks?"

"Hmmm...yeah, but it's not going to be super sweet, is it?"

"No, no. I'll put a lot of ice in it. You'll see how delicious it'll be."

"Say, you sure have a lot of CD's to choose from... Who's this guy?"

"Let's see... Oh, he's a singer from...from one of the islands in the Indian Ocean."

"Really? So what's it like?"

"Put in on if you want."

"O.K."

"I'm really happy you're here, Arturo."

"Yeah?"

"Yes, of course. Besides, you already know that. Come

here—let's toast."

"Wait a minute..."

"You don't know how long I've wished for this moment."

"Why?"

"Because... You know, Arturo; I've already told you a million times: I really like you...I...I find you quite attractive and...and I'm beginning to have feelings for you. You make me hot, as they say. Come here...Cheers."

"Cheers."

"I can tell you're a little nervous. Why? Don't you trust me?"

"Sure, it's not that."

"Then relax. You're at home, and don't think I'm just saying that: you can consider this your home. Do whatever you'd like."

"O.K., then I'm going to go to sleep. Ha ha."

"Come here."

"I don't like this music. Can I change it? It sounds like something the maids would listen to."

"Well, it's pop music—what were you expecting? I never said it was great music."

"So can I put on something else?"

"Leave it on for just a minute. Come here."

"Oh, Santiago."

"Come here, or I'm going to go over there."

"Take it easy, all right?"

"I want to be close to you. Is there something wrong with that?"

"No, but...wait a minute, man."

"Don't be afraid of me. I'm not going to hurt you. My only wish is for you to be happy... to feel at ease here in your home. Are you uncomfortable?"

"No, no."

"You're sweating, Arturo."

"Well, that's because it's really hot, Santiago."

"Don't try to be coy with me, all right? I know what's wrong, Arturo."

"So what's wrong?"

"Well, it's that...in spite of your personality—your apparent self-assuredness—you don't have much experience in this."

"That could be."

"That's natural; you're very young... Maybe I'm your first experience...or one of your first experiences—is that possible?"

"Yeah."

"I also had my first experience when I was about your age; isn't that just how life is?"

"..."

"Don't be afraid, Arturo. Nothing bad is going to happen to you while you're with me. The only risk that you run is receiving too much love—so much so you won't know what to do with it all. Besides, you can only...only wind up winning."

"Oh, my love, how wonderful you feel. Do you like this?"

"No...it's hurts, Santiago. Maybe it would be better if I were in you."

"Wait a while, my king."

"It hurts."

"Relax a little bit. I won't move. Relax."

"Ow, it hurts."

"Don't think about the pain. Think about something else, and you'll see in a while you won't feel anything. You'll even start to enjoy it. Relax."

"Ow."

"Think about something else... Think about, for example, that... What do you think about taking a trip together?"

"Where?"

"Where would you like to go?"

"I don't know. New York."

"Well then, let's go to New York. Imagine we're already there."

"It still hurts, Santiago."

"But not as bad, does it? Imagine we're in New York and...and that it's six in the evening and...and we're in a bar—your favorite bar. We're in a bar having a martini. Do you like martinis?"

"Yeah, more or less."

"Well, we're having a martini and...later that night we're going to see a play. We're relaxed, resting a little, getting back our strength... We're exhausted because we spent all day shopping... Does it hurt less?"

"Uh-huh."

"Well, don't think about it, and you'll see in just a moment the pain will go away... We're going to see a play you picked...Or maybe we're going to a rock concert to see your favorite group... Oh, my love, this really feels great, my king... I like everything about you... I really like your ass cheeks...round and hard...your smooth back...Oh, and this right here; quite surprising, isn't it? Who would believe it... I thought that it would be a lot smaller."

"Why?"

"I don't know. Well, maybe because they say when someone has a great ass, they don't have such a great dick, or vice versa, because as the saying goes, 'total bliss doesn't exist'...but you're the exception, my love—everything about you is just great."

"Really?"

"Yes, I really like you."

"It almost doesn't hurt any more. Keep talking to me."

"You're completely delicious, super tasty... You've really got a great ass—did you buy it wholesale? You don't know how hot your ass cheeks make me... They make me want to gobble them up... Give me your mouth—kiss me... Oh, my king, how happy you make me... Now you're really enjoying it, aren't you?"

"Yeah."

"It doesn't hurt anymore?"

"No."

"You're also really turned-on. Your dick is rock hard. Oh, I'd really like to suck on it right now, really deep throat you."

"Wait, don't pull out."

"You're really enjoying it, aren't you, you little fucker."

"Yeah."

"And what about this...if I push it in all the way...do you like it like that?"

"Oh yeah."

"It feels really good, my king. Tell me you feel great."

"I feel great."

"Now you talk to me."

"I really like you inside of me, Santiago."

"But don't say my name. Say, 'I really like it when you stick it all in, you fucker'."

"I really like it when you stick it all in, you fucker."

"Yeah, like that. Tell me what else."

"I like your huge dick, fucker. Oh, it feels so good. Stick in me even deeper, fucker."

"Like that, pig?"

"Yeah, like that... Oh, I'm getting ready to come."

"Then come."

"Oh...Oh..."

"I'm going to come also."

"Yeah."

"Oh, baby... Oh, it feels so good... Oh, my king, I'm coming..."

9

"Arturo?"

"Yeah, what's wrong?"

"Does it bother you that I'm calling you again?"

"No, but I thought we were done talking."

"It's just that I wanted to keep on hearing your voice."

"Oh."

"Who knows what you did to me, Arturo; I only want to be with you, talk to you."

"You're going to get bored of me."

"No, how can you even think that? You're the most important thing to me. In fact, you're the *only* thing that matters to me."

"..."

"You didn't tell me how you were dressed."

"That's why you called me?"

"No, not for that but *also* for that."

"Oh, I'm wearing some green pants and a blue T-shirt with green stripes."

"Hmmm, I bet you really look handsome."

"I guess."

"Did you mother get back?"

"No, she called a little while ago...she was going to check out a spot to shoot a commercial."

"How inconsiderate of her! I don't know how she can leave you alone for such a long period of time."

"Don't be so foolish—it's not like I'm a five-year-old kid."

"If I were her, I wouldn't take my eyes off of you."

"She doesn't...."

"You're an appetizing mouthful for anyone...a temptation for men and women. A meringue no one could resist the temptation to taste."

"Don't be so corny."

"I'm serious. You're irresistible... The driver has never come on to you?"

"What are you talking about? He's super butch."

"So how do you know that?"

"Well, you can just tell, right? He never talks about anything except chicks."

"Guys like him are the worse kind."

"He's quite a stud. It seems like he's already gotten all the chicks around here pregnant."

"Oh yeah sure, he's probably a superman."

"Haven't you checked him out? He's got a huge package!"

"Hey, hey, you're pretty observant. I'm going to get jealous."

"I don't see why. I'm not telling you I like him."

"But you just said you've noticed what a big package he has."

"It's not that I noticed. I don't find him attractive at all. It's just that he makes you notice."

"How so?"

"He's always adjusting himself, scratching himself—even in front of women."

"Incredible, isn't it? That kind of thing only happens here in Mexico."

"Really?"

"Yes, in other countries people are much more refined."

"I wonder if 'refined' is the right word."

"Seriously...foreigners, especially foreign women, when they come to Mexico, they feel very offended by that type of thing, and they're not without reason the way I see it."

"Maybe it's the other way around—they act like it bothers them when deep down they really like it."

"No, no, not at all. It's another kind of sensibility—more puritanical if you want, but... I believe you have to have respect for the tourist—in the end, they're great for the country, don't you think?"

"I don't know. I'm not interested in politics."

"Well, I'm not really interested in politics either, but I think you have to be informed—whatever happens affects all of us. We don't live in isolation..."

"..."

"I see this topic is boring you."

"That's right."

"Then let's stop talking about it, all right? We can go back to my favorite topic."

"Again?"

"Yes... Seriously, Arturo, this morning when you left, I felt a little strange, sad, as if I weren't centered... Later I realized what was really happening was I was missing you."

"But we had just seen each other."

"That may be true; even so, I was missing you. I need you, Arturo. Time feels eternal without you."

"Maybe what you need is to work—don't you think? Or find something to entertain you."

"No, it's not that...I have a lot of things to do around here... The only thing I need right now for me to be completely happy is you."

"Really?"

"Really. I feel bad when you're not with me... I become very insecure... I don't know why, but I get terrible jealously pangs. I imagine..."

"What do you imagine?"

"No, don't pay attention to me. It's silly. There's no reason for me to become a bother to you because of my insecurities... Oh, Arturo, you don't know how much I would like it if we could live together..."

"..."

"You don't think you'd like to?"

"I don't know. I haven't ever lived with anyone that way."

"Yes, I know you haven't lived with anyone, but would you like to or not?"

"Possibly."

"I would completely respect you—I'd let you do whatever you wanted. Don't think I'd constantly be bothering you. If I lived with you, I wouldn't feel so insecure, and...well, things would be different. Why don't you think about it?"

"O.K."

"Oh my God—I'm so stupid."

"Why?"

"See what you make me think about. It's with good reason they say love clouds your reasoning—here I am suggesting to you that we live together, and...I have forgotten completely about Sarita."

"And what does she have to do with anything? Do you also want her to come live with you?"

"No, no, no; why would you say that? The thing is... Well, we can't forget about her, ignore her like she didn't exist... After all, she and I have been friends for many years."

"And so what? Would it spoil your good mood if she got mad?"

"I don't know if 'spoil my good mood' is the right expression. Maybe it would hurt me. Once, our friendship was...was on hold. I wouldn't like it if the same thing happened now...I'm no longer...I don't know—I'm no longer at an age to make enemies."

"That doesn't have anything to do with age."

"Yes, I think it does. When you're older, you should try to make up with your enemies and not...not awaken hostilities."

"Whatever—maybe you'll have to choose."

"Between her and you?"

"Uh-huh."

"Well, you, definitely, but it doesn't have to do with that. I just want to make sure to continue to have Sarita's friendship."

"'Total bliss doesn't exist' as you like to say."

"Yes, you're right... Everything is so difficult, isn't it?"

"More or less."

"I don't want to hurt her again either."

"This isn't going to hurt her, Santiago. If she can't deal with this, it's because she's an idiot—I don't believe she thinks I'm going to live with her forever."

"No, no, of course not, but... Am I to understand because of what you're saying you're going to accept my proposition that we live together?"

"Possibly—I'm fed up with living at home."

"That's great news, Arturo. You don't know how happy you've just made me."

"But, it doesn't seem that way. You sound kind of worried to me."

"Well, you know the only thing that worries me is Sarita."

"What a total drag—we always end up talking about her."

"All right—I promise not to mention her again. I don't want my...my worries, my reservations to rub off on you either. I'll think of something."

"O.K."

"In the final analysis, you're much more mature than I am, Arturo. You confront things with more practicality... Well, I won't take up more of your time. Wish me a good night."

"Have a good evening, Santiago even though it's not going to help at all—you're still not going to be able to sleep."

"Why do you say that?"

"Because I know you—you're going to be tossing and turning all night long thinking about the thing with my mother."

"I promise I'll only do that for a short while—until I find the solution."

"O.K. then."

"Until tomorrow, Arturo."

"Ciao."

10

"Oh, Arturo, I'm really worried. Do you think Sarita might know something?"

"About what?"

"About us. Do you think she could have heard some rumor?"

"Why do you ask?"

"Well, because she called to tell me she wanted to talk to me. These things make me very nervous. Any time someone says they want to talk to me, I imagine the worst. This is awful. I don't know how I'm going to deal with this situation."

"But was she angry or what?"

"No, no...not at all—she sounded fine to me."

"Then it was probably about something else, the investments for example."

"It can't be about the investments—that's already taken care of."

"Or for something else."

"But what?"

"There's nothing weird about her wanting to talk to you; she's your friend, isn't she?"

"Don't even remind me about that right now—I feel badly about her...as if I had betrayed her."

"Calm down, man...so when are you going to see her?"

"Tomorrow. We agreed to have dinner."

"Oh."

"But before that, I'd like to see you so you can give me courage. Could we see each other today?"

"Oh, Santiago, you're getting carried away."

"Well, I didn't want to see you just because of that. I also want to see you because I desire you, because I adore you, because you drive me crazy."

"You're getting carried away again."

"No, my love, no. I love you very much."

"Well, where do you want to meet?"

"Is my house all right?"

"Yeah, but why don't we have dinner before that?"

"If you want to, but... I don't know—maybe that's not a good idea—someone could see us."

"Oh, Santiago."

"We could order something in. What would you like to eat?"

"Hamburgers."

"Wouldn't you prefer something more...refined?"

"Oh, don't be so corny—you're just like my mother."

"No, no, you'll see. I'm thinking about something you're going to love."

"O.K., but you have to take me to eat hamburgers another day."

"Yes, my love, whenever you'd like."

II

"You're really getting into it, aren't you, you little fucker."

"Yeah."

"It doesn't hurt anymore does it?"

"Hardly at all."

"You're becoming more and more of a little faggot, aren't you? You really like a big dick up your ass."

"..."

"It wasn't really that difficult for you to get used to it, was it?"

"It still hurts just a little."

"But you like it more than it hurts you, isn't that right, you little fucker?"

"Uh-huh."

"Oh, my love, this feels so good...I'm about to come... You come also."

"Yeah."

"Oh, oh, oh, my king...oh...oh..."

"Hold on—don't pull out—I'm getting ready to come."

"Shoot, my love, shoot."

"..."

"Finished?"

"Yeah."

"Did you shoot a huge load?"

"Yeah, and you?"

"Oh yes, me too. Look how you left me... I can hardly breathe... Let's see, I'm going to give you something so you can get cleaned up... Stay there if you want... Rest; don't move... Take this..."

"Thanks."

"..."

"..."

"Say, Arturo, am I really the first guy to be inside you?"

"Yeah."

"I don't believe you."

"Why not?"

"Because it's not possible... It's not possible ...nowadays...with you being so good-looking...that you haven't had other opportunities."

"I'm not saying I haven't had other opportunities."

"Then?"

"You asked me if someone else had been inside me, didn't you? Well no, no one has been inside me."

"Why not?"

"Because I didn't think it was worth it."

"But you do with me?"

"More or less."

"Hey, hey, what do you mean, 'more or less?' You should have said, 'Yes, it sure is worth it with you'."

"I was joking, man."

"You've never given up your ass to anyone?"

"No, don't you believe me?"

"Yes, sure I believe you, my love. Besides, I can tell— you're still very tight... I love the way you squeeze me."

"..."

"But you've had sexual relations with others, haven't you?"

"No."

"I don't believe you, Arturo—it's just not possible."

"It's true even if you don't believe me."

"Really? Not with anyone?"

"Uh-uh."

"You're not lying to me?"

"Oh, you're annoying me again, Santiago."

"No, forgive me, my love; I don't want to nag you, but it just seems inconceivable to me."

"Well, that's the way it is."

"Never? You didn't do anything with anybody?"

"Uh-uh."

"Not even when you were much younger, with your friends?"

"Well, yeah, with a cousin, when I was twelve-years-old, but nothing at all happened. We just touched each other a little bit."

"And besides him, anyone else?"

"No one."

"Oh, Arturo, you don't know how happy it makes me to be the first man in your life—seriously my love."

"That's good."

"I know for you it's not important, but for me it is... Look, Arturo, how things are—I had a feeling this was going to happen. I knew life had this present in store for me."

"Why do you say that, huh?"

"Well, because...I don't know; I've always believed life was just, fair; that the good things one does have a payback. Of course, the bad ones do too... It's just that you can't appreciate the effect of your actions until later."

"And what does that have to do with me?"

"Well, that's what I was going to tell you. When I was your age—or more or less your age—I...I told you my first experience was with a man much older than I, didn't I?"

"Uh-huh."

"Well listen to this Arturo—when I was with him I thought, 'This situation will repeat itself in my life, only it will be reversed—when I'm as old as he is, I'm going to have a very important relationship with someone much younger than me.' It seemed inevitable to me—and you see—that's exactly what happened. What do you think about that?"

"Well, to me it just seems like a coincidence. I mean, what if I hadn't wanted to?"

"I would have insisted. I would have insisted until you gave in. You weren't going to get away so easily."

"Well, but if after insisting a lot, I still wouldn't have wanted to, what would you have done?"

"Well..."

"You would have found someone else, wouldn't you? Someone who was my same age so you could fulfill your prophecy."

"Hey, that's not true at all. You're very close to saying I'm a dirty old man. No. You're the one who got my attention. I am particularly interested in *you*—not just some young guy around your age."

"But what would you have done then?"

"I don't know. I'm sure I would have accepted the situation calmly. I don't know. Fortunately, reality coincided with my desires and... Thanks Arturo... Thanks for giving me everything you do."

12

"Hold on to your seat, Arturo—I have some great news for you!"

"What?"

"Are you sitting down?"

"Yeah, well actually I'm lying down. Why do you ask? Do you want me to tell you how I'm dressed?"

"No, no. I'm going to give you a surprise."

"You're going to give me a car!"

"No, it's not that. You don't have any idea what it could be?"

"No."

"We're going to live together, Arturo! It's almost a done deal."

"What did you say?"

"Exactly what you just heard—we're going to live together—and with your mother's blessing!"

"Hey, but... I told you I wasn't sure if I wanted to live with you."

"Yes, of course. Don't think I've forgotten you haven't given me a definite answer yet, but...well, it's just that things turned out in such a way that... Let me tell you how everything happened."

"All right, tell me."

"Well, look, actually, Sarita didn't know anything about us. She didn't even suspect."

"And you told her everything?"

"No, no; what are you thinking? Hold on a second. The reason Sarita wanted to see me was because...well, to say it another way, she wanted to complain about you to me."

"Oh, what an idiot."

"She told me she was really worried because you weren't going to school...she didn't like the type of friends you were making, and she didn't know what to do about it. She saw your future as very uncertain."

"Oh."

"She wanted me to give her some advice."

"And what did you tell her?"

"Well, that... You'll have to give me credit, Arturo. I handled everything with a great deal of tact and skill."

"But what did you tell her?"

"I told her...what she needed to do wasn't to pressure you; she shouldn't force you to study something, but rather...well, to let you decide for yourself."

"And...?"

"Of course she didn't agree. You know how Sarita is— she likes to have her own way, but then I told her one way of respecting your decisions was to offer you various options—one of them was for her to help you start up a small business."

"How awful!"

"Yes, she didn't think it was a good idea either. Another option was to stop giving you money."

"Thanks for your help, Santiago."

"Hey, don't use that tone. If I told her that, it was because I didn't want her to suspect I was on your side."

"So then what happened?"

"And the third option, which is the one she liked best and the one that concerns you and me, was for you to keep studying but in a different way."

"What a crock!"

"No, no, wait a second. I told her if she wanted to see a change in your studies, if she wanted to get you away from your friends who surely had a bad influence on you, what she needed to do was to send you abroad to study something that would interest you."

"Oh, but why do I have to study something?"

"Hold on, my love; we'll talk about that afterwards. Let me finish telling you what we talked about... At the beginning, Sarita didn't really agree—she told me she didn't have the necessary means to..."

"You see how stingy she is? Do you believe she couldn't afford that for me?"

"Hold on, my love. Then I told her there was always a way to solve things, right? I explained maybe you could get a scholarship or financial aid. I told her I had contacts at the University of Houston, and I could look into that if she wanted. And it was then that her eyes began to light up...she began thinking about what I was dying for her to ask me—that you could go live there with me in my home. She told me she would only agree if you went with someone whom she completely trusted—like me—who could exercise a certain control over you—someone who wasn't going to let you just run wild."

"Oh, you think you're so smart."

"'Listen, Sarita; that's a huge responsibility,' I told her. 'Do you realize what you're asking me'?"

"And what did she say to that?"

"That yes, she understood, that she completely trusted me and she knew because of the fondness I have for her I would take good care of you, almost as if it were she whom I was taking care of."

"Oh."

"So what do you think, my love? Maybe this old guy who loves you so much is pretty cool after all?"

"Why 'cool'?"

"Because I managed to get the best for everyone without having to ask for it. There was even a moment when Sarita insisted on it. She told me to think about it and... Well, she asked me to do it for her to help her solve this problem."

"And what did you tell her?"

"I told her I would think about it and that she could count on me. I said if I couldn't resolve the problem directly, I would find a way for someone to take charge. I asked her to leave everything to me."

"You see? You're not so stupid, Santiago."

"Really? Anyway I told her it was you who had to decide so it wouldn't seem like she and I were planning your life without taking you into consideration—or like we were manipulating you."

"Man, well thanks for letting me give my opinion."

"No, don't take it like that, my love. Try to see the positive side."

"And what's the positive side?"

"Well, this way everyone wins—Sarita will calm down because you're going to do something; I'm going to be immensely happy about having you by my side, and you...well, it's not so bad for you either."

"Why? I'm going to have to study really hard, won't I?"

"Yes, but you'll get other things in exchange, Arturo."

"What things?"

"You'll have my unconditional love. You won't lack for anything. Listen carefully: nothing. And you know I tend to be generous with my loved ones. Besides...well...besides we're going to be able to take a lot of trips, have a great time, and love each other. Does that seem like so little?"

"No."

"Anyway, let Sarita be the one who brings this up. She told me she was going to talk to you. And you, don't give in right away. Make her beg a little so she won't suspect we had already planned this."

"O.K."

"Oh, my love, we're going to be so happy!"

Two

OCTOBER

"She called again?"

"Yes."

"And what did she want?"

"Nothing special—just to say hello and see how we were."

"How annoying."

"Yes, even I have to admit she's a bit insistent, but deep down I think she's right to call...maybe if I were her I'd do the same thing."

"That's because you are a bit insistent too, but that doesn't mean you all are right. What a way to be a fucking nuisance!"

"Hey, hey, show some more respect please. If you don't respect Sarita—and believe me I understand your reasons—at least respect me because..."

"Because why? Because you're the one who supports me?"

"No, my love; I didn't say that. Why would you say such a thing?"

"But you thought it, didn't you?"

"I certainly did not. What I was going to say is you should respect me since I'm your partner. If you don't respect your own partner, who are you going to respect?"

"Do you really think I don't respect you?"

"No, no, my love; I don't think that. It's just a way of speaking. I said that because...well, it just didn't seem like a good idea for you to say...well, I don't like that you confuse worry or...or concern with wanting to be a fucking nuisance."

"Well, sure, but there are ways of worrying about people without being such a drag. My mother already knows I'm all right, doesn't she? She says she trusts you, doesn't she? Then why does she have to be calling all the time?"

"Well, it's just that Sarita, in spite of always seeming so in control, is really rather insecure when you get right down to it. Who knows why, but that's just the way she is. I'm sure she thinks if she doesn't have everything under control, if she's not supervising everything constantly, something is going to go wrong. Maybe she's like that because of her job. She has the responsibility of managing a lot of people and of making sure everything turns out well. The weight she has to carry around on her shoulders is too much. It makes sense, doesn't it? I've never thought about that before now."

"Do you really think so? So she wasn't like that before?"

"Let's just say she had the potential, but it hadn't been fully developed. She used to be more flexible before— well, in one sense. She also had her tantrums, but she allowed herself to go with the flow more easily... Now, in that sense, she's a bit more rigid...but yes, if I really think about it, she was always a little bit like that..."

"I don't know how you put up with her."

"Hey, come on. Sarita has some very positive qualities. I've learned a lot from her."

"Like what?"

"Well...like her willingness to work, her discipline. She's one of the most organized people I know. And also...well, her sense of humor is something I value a lot, plus it's really helped me. You won't believe it, but at certain times when I see things aren't going very well, I stop and think, 'What would Sarita do in this situation?', and I almost always arrive at the conclusion that she'd think of something very clever to say...you know how she doesn't take anything seriously."

"Except for herself."

"Yes, you're right. At times it's hard for her to maintain a distance from herself...a distance her sense of humor lets her have in front of others. But sometimes she is also able to make fun of herself. And believe me, humor always makes a difficult situation easier to handle."

"Agreed...although it seems to me she uses her sense of humor to cover up her real feelings—she's always agonizing."

"Another thing I like about Sarita is her sensitivity and her ability to seduce. You got that from her. Maybe you don't realize it, but you are also very seductive—everyone easily falls into your web."

"And is that bad?"

"No, no, on the contrary, I'm saying it's one of the reasons why I admire her."

"And that you learned from her, too?"

"Oh, I don't know about that, but I certainly give her credit."

"It seems to me you give her too much credit; you can't see her...what's the word I'm looking for?"

"Objectively?"

"Uh-huh. You can't see her objectively. She really has impressed you—I don't know why; after all the time you've known her, she still impresses you. It's as if you had just met her."

"That's not true. I can recognize Sarita's defects, too. Her...her own insistence is one of them. It's just that, for me—maybe because I respect her—her positive qualities are more important."

"Oh."

"I mean in general, I always pay more attention to the positive qualities of someone than their defects. We all have our weak spot, don't you think? I don't see why one can't forgive weaknesses in others."

"I didn't say you shouldn't forgive them. What I'm saying is you only see the things you like about a person—you don't see the rest."

"Well, it's a way to be positive about life, don't you think?"

"Maybe, but I don't think that's good...it's like feeling inferior to everyone else."

"Really? No. Why do you say that?"

"Because you see them as bigger than they really are."

"No, no, I insist..."

"Well, don't insist."

"Let me finish. I think all virtues are...they're just as important as the defects. They balance them out. For every bad thing someone has, they also have something good... Look, let me make a proposal—you'll see I'm right. You name one of Sarita's defects, and I'll give you a positive quality that corresponds to it, all right?"

"O.K."

"What is her most serious defect in your opinion?"

"Her most serious defect is that she's a complete drag."

"No, no, try to say that another way."

"She's a complete drag."

"Fine, but try to be specific as to what you mean by that."

"She's always a pain in the ass...really insistent."

"I agree she's insistent, but do you know why she's so insistent? Because she's capable of giving a lot of love. And there is her positive quality: if she's bothersome to others— to you—for example, it's because she loves you so much."

"Uh, I'd prefer for her to love me less."

"Hey, listen to me—don't say that."

"Well, another defect is that she's very demanding."

"Well it's for the same reason—she asks a lot because she gives so much."

"Oh, come on; that doesn't count—you have to find some other positive quality she has...and if you can't, this is all a big joke."

"Well, she's generous—she gives herself to others. She's generous with her time and with her attention and..."

"But not with her money."

"Well, that's another topic, but she sometimes even sacrifices her needs to give to others."

"Are you sure you're talking about my mother?"

"Yes, yes...of course. Look, in that regard, I've seen every little detail..."

"Well, I've also seen every little detail but in another way—for example, the business about the Cokes."

"What Cokes?"

"What I already told you, man—she keeps the Cokes under lock and key so the maids don't drink them...and the cookies and the coffee and the canned goods. Everything. Everything in the pantry."

"Well, but in that regard—also in that regard—she's not wrong."

"Let's see then; why don't you keep your pantry locked up?"

"Well, because... It's different; look—people are hungrier there, aren't they? You can't leave everything out within their reach. They're voracious...they're like termites."

"Yeah, but not even I can take things from the pantry only during meals. That seems all right with you?"

"Well, what you consider a defect also has its positive side: organization, order. If you went around eating sweets all day long, maybe your stomach would hurt, or you'd ruin your teeth, or..."

"Or I wouldn't be such a stud, right?"

"Exactly. You said it...maybe my partner would be a little chubby."

"Anyway, it still seems to me it's a stingy thing, or are you going to say my mother isn't stingy?"

"I don't see it like that."

"Oh, Santiago, you really are very naive. Look, I'm going to tell you something so you can see for yourself how stingy she is. She's capable of anything as long as it doesn't have to do with spending. One day Octavio invited her out to eat—you know Octavio, don't you?"

"Yes."

"Well, the day he invited her out to eat, she told him she was going to bring me also since there wasn't anyone at home, and that she was going to pay for me, got it? ...so Octavio wouldn't feel like she was taking advantage of him or that it was, um, what's the word?"

"An imposition."

"Uh-huh. And Octavio told her sure, of course, but not to bring any money...there wouldn't be any need to. On the contrary, he would be pleased to pay for me as well."

"Well, so far, I see everything as perfectly normal. I don't find any reason for criticizing Sarita's behavior."

"Hold on. That's when my mother insisted and kept on insisting she was going to pay for me so Octavio would think my mother was really cool and everything, right? And there you have it...after insisting repeatedly, Octavio accepted. Then we left the house, all right? and when we were getting into Octavio's car, one of the maids came up to her and asked her if she couldn't give her some money since she had to go to the supermarket. And then my mother said, 'Oh Vianey, why are you asking me about money now?' And the maid answered, 'But ma'am, you told me to remind you to give me some money before you left.' And she opened up her purse and gave her everything she had, right?, which, by the way, wasn't very much."

"Well, that doesn't prove anything, Arturo—that could happen to anyone...we can all be caught unprepared at any time, don't you think?"

"Yeah, but not her. I'm sure she had planned everything, that she had told the maid to ask her for money when we were getting into the car so she wouldn't have to go back for more money, and that way she wouldn't have to pay for dinner."

"Oh come on; I don't think Sarita is so calculating, so Machiavellian."

"Well, maybe she didn't say it like that, but she did say, 'Don't forget to ask me for the money before I go'...that's more her style—to do things without calling attention to them, and that way she looks good to everyone, doesn't she? For example, with Octavio—she came out looking just fine to him because it wasn't so obvious she wanted to get him to pay for me."

"I wonder."

"And there wasn't any problem with the servant because my mom gave her the money for the supermarket. Plus my mom looked good in my eyes because she made it seem like she was worried about me...that I wouldn't end up not eating."

"Well, you're giving me something to think about, but I don't believe it. You have to be very malicious, very... That's what I mean when I tell you you're too intelligent, Arturo."

"But do you know who she really looked good to? With herself because in the end she didn't spend anything, and she got her way."

"Nothing gets by you. In that way you're like Sarita who analyzes everything from all possible angles."

"Oh, don't fuck with me... You haven't noticed what my

mother is like when you talk to her on the phone?"

"What do you mean haven't I noticed?"

"Yeah. You've never noticed anything strange?"

"No."

"I have, but the thing is for you to notice. Come on...what's my mother like when she talks on the phone?"

"Well, the same as always: effusive, um...warm; at times a little excessive, but she is also excessive when you're face to face with her."

"No, I'm not talking about that. Haven't you noticed something else? Something that has to do with how long her phone calls last?"

"No. Well, in that regard, she's just like everyone else—sometimes she makes brief calls, and sometimes she makes longer calls."

"And haven't you noticed what that depends on?"

"I suppose on how much time she has or her mood—just like everyone else, don't you think?"

"No. Pay attention next time: it depends on who calls. If someone calls her, she'll stay on the line for hours, but if she's the one who calls, then she only talks for a few minutes."

"Seriously?"

"Yeah—when she calls, she's always in a hurry and only says what she absolutely has to, but when someone calls her, she explains everything in great detail, and she starts talking about her problems and everything because she isn't the one who's paying for the call."

"Well, you are certainly determined to get me to think Sarita is a stingy person."

"Do you know how far she'll go at times when she needs to talk to someone?"

"No."

"She dials the number, and when someone answers, right

away she says to them, 'My dear, I have to hang up right now because—whatever—but could you call me in fifteen minutes'?"

"Oh, I don't believe you, ha ha. You're making me laugh."

"So you think it's funny?"

"Well, truthfully, yes. It seems like this is one of your exaggerations, a product of your sense of humor. And don't think I'm not delighted you're like that."

"Pay close attention next time so you see it's not one of my exaggerations."

"If she were like what you've described, she wouldn't call us so often."

"Undoubtedly she's calling from work because she can call for free...or from an office, or I don't know...or, let's see, why doesn't she ever call at night when the rates are cheaper?"

"Well, you're right about that, ha ha."

"You see?"

"Well, whatever the case, Sarita's stinginess, as you call it, is compensated by her ingenuity...by her ability to get things to turn out well, without difficulty. That has its merit—don't you think? So ultimately everything balances out."

"Another thing is she feels she's very important."

"You say that as a defect? Maybe it's not a defect, Arturo. Sarita is an exceptional person. Perhaps she values herself for what she is—someone out of the ordinary."

"She's always talking about the people she knows, about everyone who owes her a favor, about the influence she has on people."

"And isn't that true? Be objective, Arturo—it's obvious to me—you don't know how many people acknowledge the importance she has had in their lives."

"To begin with—you."

"Yes, to a certain degree, but there are those people for

whom Sarita's influence has been decisive. Look, I've found that... During the time Sarita and I were distant with one another, at some get-togethers, I found some people—especially women—had the unmistakable influence of Sarita in their gestures and..."

"What a bunch of shit!"

"And in their behavior, in the way they expressed themselves, and at that moment, I swear I would have put my hand in the fire to be certain they were friends of Sarita, or at least they knew her and admired her."

"Oh really?"

"Yes, exactly. And later, talking to them, I confirmed it. They were like duplicates of Sarita—some even had the same phobias, the same compulsions, the same... Suddenly, they seemed a little pathetic, don't you think?"

"What do you mean 'pathetic'?"

"Well, it's someone you feel sorry for, right? Someone who... A pathetic person is a person who seems ridiculous and who you feel sorry for all at the same time—you know what I'm saying?"

"Like my mother."

"No, no, not at all. Sarita is not pathetic. It's those who try to imitate her who are pathetic, like every imitator, like every copy. There's always something sad in any copy. Sarita, on the other hand, has the advantage of being very original."

"And can't you be original and pathetic?"

"No, I don't think so."

"Because, according to your definition, it seems to me my mother is pathetic."

"Why?"

"Because of her need to show she's very important, that everyone pays attention to her when at times they don't even gossip about her. If she were really so important, she wouldn't have to show it, would she? She would be able to let others speak positively about her, but she wouldn't always have to insist all the time about how important she is."

"The thing is Sarita is very sensitive and therefore very insecure. That's why she has to reaffirm herself in front of others at times."

"At *times?*"

"All right, very frequently."

"She *always* has to be showing off...you don't think that's pathetic?"

"You really like that word, didn't you? Not a day passes you don't learn something, as the saying goes."

"But seriously, isn't that pathetic? She always has to prove she's perfect in everything she does."

"Well, I don't think you can criticize her for being a perfectionist. On the contrary, we need more people like her in Mexico. If everyone were like her, we'd be a first world country."

"But she's not like that just in her job. She's like that as a human being. It always seems she's acting for others—for example, when someone comes over. It always seems she's doing something that's very well rehearsed so as to impress people."

"I don't understand. Let's see, can you give me an example?"

"It's what I was just saying—her way with people, the things she talks about. She always has to give a very flattering impression of herself, and that's what seems so false to me. I'm sure when someone is going to come over to the house, she thinks about what things she can say to impress them, what she should serve them for dinner, or whatever to impress them—got it? Or when she's about to get into the car. I don't believe she can relax until she thinks of the phrase for the day or a joke."

"Oh, ha ha; you're heartless, Arturo."

"But that's what she's like—I'm serious. Look, when someone is going to come over to the house, she puts on makeup, she tries on one dress, then another; she puts on a brooch, then another one, she looks at herself in the mirror. I've even caught her making gestures in the mirror, and that's the way it always has to be. The thing is I've been able to watch her in the house—all of it is so studied. Of course the funny thing is she doesn't realize she's acting."

"Well, but even with her histrionics, if you look at it from another angle, it could be a virtue and not a defect. It also seems to me it's a sign of generosity to think about others, to make sure they have a nice time, an interesting time, or why not a really fun time?"

"Then she should be a clown in a circus."

"That's not true. If you think about it, every great personality is somewhat, well...studied, as you say. Of course, to each his own, but what unites all of them is they are people who, at one moment in their lives, have made the decision to create themselves, to work on their personality, to polish it in every detail until it is more in line with their wishes. Look, it's like a female writer used to say: you have to construct yourself, create a personality— you can't leave everything to nature. Nature also produces monsters—don't believe everything that is natural is good. And then...well, in any construction there's already a human element, don't you think? Something worked on, something artificial. And maybe that's what's leading you to believe Sarita is false. What's actually happening is that you're confusing being artificial with being false, and they're not the same. What's artificial has to do with art. The very word even says it: *art*-ificial."

"I think I'm going to go."

"Wait just a second. Why are you in such a hurry? Don't you want some more tea?"

"No, not any more."

"Don't tell me it's already time for you to get going."

"No, but I want to go look at some CD's."

"And why don't you wait and we can go together tomorrow? I wanted to buy some music also."

"Oh, Santiago."

"Come on, my love. Be a good little boy and wait until tomorrow so we can both go."

"O.K."

"Or are you in a particular hurry?"

"No."

"Because if you are, I don't want to pressure you, my love,...speaking of impositions, right? That would be very irresponsible of me."

"No, I'll wait."

"That way we can buy some other little something, all right? Something you really want."

"O.K."

"I need to buy some things also. I want to see if I can find a mouse trap."

"Are there mice here? I'm getting out of this house, is that clear?"

"Oh, my love, it's only one mouse, and it's only this big...look. Don't be scared."

"But where did it come from?"

"Well... I found it in the attic."

"Oh, Santiago, then they must be in every part of the house."

"No, my love. I'm telling you there is only one. Say, I didn't know you were afraid of mice. I thought you weren't afraid of anything."

"How do you know there's only one?"

"Because I checked carefully."

"Oh, Santiago."

"Really, my love. There's only one—in the attic."

"Why don't you fumigate? There have to be more."

"No, my love; please believe me."

"How gross!"

"I think it probably came from the neighbor's house. You know how our dear little neighbor is. All of a sudden they've opened a sleazy hotel you don't like."

"What a bunch of pigs."

"Don't start acting rude to them, Arturo. I don't want to have problems with anyone, much less the neighbors."

"I don't intend to be nice or rude to them, and that's that. End of story."

"Really, who knows why some people are like that? They can move to another neighborhood, to another city, even to another country—like these people did; they can even change their social status...but what they bring with them from birth, that they can't change."

"You think so?"

"Well, yes—can't you see for yourself? And it's not because they don't have money, Arturo. Those people have a lot of money. The thing is...well, your upbringing determines a lot, don't you think? If these people had been born in another environment, they would be very different... If for no other reason you should at least be grateful to Sarita for the education she gave you."

"Come on! Are we going to start talking about her again?"

"Seriously, Arturo: your upbringing is your best inheritance."

"Well, I'd prefer to get another type of inheritance."

"Really, my love, one day you're going to remember what I'm telling you: what Sarita has taught you from the way she has raised you—and why not say it? Her very example is the most valuable thing you have. Some day you'll realize that—you'll see."

"O.K., but until that day comes we can continue to speak badly of her."

"We can? I don't think so—I will not speak badly of Sarita. I only have good things to say about her."

"You won't speak badly, but you really like it when I criticize her. Don't think I haven't noticed."

"Well, it's always more fun to talk badly of someone, or hear bad things about someone than to speak well of somebody. Besides, it's more constructive: if you observe the errors of those who surround you, it's more likely you can avoid committing them."

"That's true."

"Seriously, my love...look, everything you say about Sarita, everything that bothers you, I pay careful attention to so as not to commit the same mistakes with you."

"Now you're really talking like my mother."

"How's that?"

"Well, you're...how would you say it? You're explaining something so it's helpful to you—you're justifying yourself."

"No, my love—not at all."

"You always manipulate everything so you can use it to your advantage, don't you think?"

"Is that what it seems like to you?"

"She's deceitful. She's capable of anything so she gets her way. She's the one who is too intelligent. Don't tell me you haven't realized that."

"Well, skillful I'd say."

"You see? That's what I'm saying, Santiago, and you're also deceitful."

"Oh come on—why do you say that?"

"You're always finding a way to defend yourself also. And when we talk about her, you defend her."

"Then I'm too intelligent also?"

"Skillful I'd say.'"

"No, Arturo; I'm not trying to defend myself or to defend her. We were playing a game, weren't we? You were telling me one of Sarita's defects, and I was trying to balance it with one of her virtues..."

"But that's how you always are—even if we're not playing."

"Besides, you can't see only negative things about your mom."

"I can too...I most certainly can—I assure you."

"But that's not good, Arturo. It's natural; don't think I don't understand. At least it's normal at your age to reject Sarita. We all have that kind of reaction at some time in our lives, but it's not good."

"It would be better if we talked about something else."

"You shouldn't try to avoid this topic."

"It's not that I'm trying to avoid it, Santiago—I'm bored with it."

"I agree, my love—let's change topics. What do you want to talk about?"

"Oh, Santiago."

"What?"

"We have to agree on what we're going to talk about?"

"Well, no, but..."

"We're not even at school."

"All right—we're going to let the conversation develop naturally."

"..."

"Come here; sit down... Give me a kiss."

"O.K."

"Oh, my love, I really feel very happy to be with you. You don't know how much I value your company."

"Me too."

"Are you serious? You half-way made a sneer."

"I'm saying I, too, really value my company."

"You see how you are?"

"But you love me this way, don't you?"

"Of course, my love... How do you feel? Do you feel all right here?"

"Yeah, but don't ask me so much if I feel all right here. You ask me that all day long, Santiago."

"Well, I'm just worried about your well-being."

"O.K., but don't be so insistent."

"You really don't miss your house, your friends?"

"Not at all, man."

"Oh, my love, who knew, right?, that at my age I would enjoy such happiness. If a, um, fortune-teller had told me ten years ago, I wouldn't have believed it."

"But didn't you sense it? Weren't you sure it was going to happen?"

"Well, I wasn't completely sure. Let's just say it's what I wanted—it's what seemed fair, but you never know what the future holds in store for you. I can now certainly say life has given me what I wanted—and then some."

"Do you think when I'm your age I'm going to go out with someone younger than me?"

"It's quite likely. I think life gives you those kind of compensations."

"Well, that's fucked up—I don't like younger guys."

"You will. I thought the same thing when I was your age. What happens is that as time passes, you begin to become interested in people younger than you. This happens to everyone; don't think it only happens to gay people. Older heterosexual men fall in love with younger women. Older women too— think about how many women go out with men who are younger than they are."

"And why's that?"

"Well, I don't know. Maybe it's a way to try to recoup lost youth, a way to find a...um, something that renews their lives. Our lives, don't you think?"

"Tell me what the first guy you went out with was like."

"I've already talked to you about that relationship, my love...about the importance it had for me."

"But you've never told me what he was like."

"Well, he was a older man but very well-preserved."

"Like you?"

"Thanks for thinking I'm well-preserved, Arturo."

"Did he look like you?"

"No, no, not at all. He was very different: dark-skinned with straight hair; it was really strange—he almost didn't have any gray hair. He had...well, for his age he was really fine. He had very muscular legs—arms too. In general, he was very gifted."

"And there?"

"He was also 'gifted' there. Come on, what a thing to be interested in, huh?"

"That's important too, isn't it? Or maybe that doesn't matter to you?"

"Let's just say it wasn't the most important thing."

"Don't pretend to be so innocent."

"Well, yes, it mattered to me—of course it did, but it wasn't everything. There were more important things. Let's just say that if his measurements had been smaller, I would have fallen in love with him anyway."

"Why?"

"Because he was a very loving man, very tender, very understanding."

"Everything is 'very'."

"Yes, although he also had defects."

"Was he jealous?"

"Yes, quite a bit."

"Like you."

"I'm not jealous, am I? Do you think I'm jealous?"

"Sometimes."

"But not as much as I used to be, right?"

"Uh-huh."

"I was jealous when I wasn't with you, and that's natural, but now I don't have any reason to be jealous, or do I?"

"Continue."

"Well, another one of his defects was that he was very insecure. In spite of his age and everything he had experienced in life and in spite of having a lot of money, he was a terribly insecure man."

"Why?"

"He had had a very difficult childhood. He missed out on a lot of things... His mother died when he was very small, and later his father married several times."

"Were you happy as a child?"

"Yes. I definitely can't complain—I had everything I needed and more."

"I didn't."

"Don't say that, Arturo. Let's see, what did you miss out on?"

"Oh, many things, but keep going."

"What more do you want me to tell you?"

"How did you guys fuck?"

"Oh come on—you don't talk about those things."

"Why not?"

"Because it's not good to talk about those things."

"Because it's bad?"

"No, no, it's not because of that. When it has to do with love, there can't be anything bad. Let's just say that it's not in good taste to talk about those things."

"That's not a good reason."

"It's not in good taste because... If it were something that happened only to me, I wouldn't have any qualms telling you about it, but from the moment someone else is involved, that's no longer the case. At that point, you're getting yourself involved in someone else's life."

"That's true."

"I can tell you, however, that in general it was a very passionate and fiery relationship."

"And were you faithful to him?"

"Come on—your question offends me. Of course I was faithful to him. I have always been a man of principles."

"Me too."

"Yes, I suppose so. In some way, the upbringing that..."

"I always like beginnings[10]: I start things but I don't ever finish them."

"You're pulling my leg again."

"Don't you value my sense of humor?"

"Yes, my love, of course I do, but..."

"Oh, I've really got to go now, all right?"

"Sure. I hope you learn a lot."

"O.K. See you later."

"But say goodbye to me properly, my love. Give me a hug. Give me a kiss."

"Uh-huh."

"Behave yourself."

"I always behave myself—you know that. Will you give

me some money? I need to get some gas for the car."

"Of course I will. Here you go."

"…"

"Be careful, all right?"

"Uh-huh. You too—remember the majority of accidents happen at home."

NOVEMBER

"Tell me about your underwear."

"I'm only wearing my briefs."

"Well, tell me what it's like."

"White, very short—they're the kind that are really skimpy and only cover my dick. You can see where my pubic hair begins."

"And from behind?"

"From behind you can easily see my ass cheeks."

"Oh, that sounds wonderful, my love."

"The only thing covered is my crack."

"Hmmm…Rub it a little bit."

"O.K."

"But tell me about it. Tell me how you're doing it."

"I'm caressing my crack. I'm sticking my fingers up my ass."

"How are you?"

"Really great."

"I already know that. I'm asking you what position you're in?"

"I'm sitting in bed...on my legs."

"Then you can't caress your crack very well."

"Yeah, I can because I've raised my ass cheeks a little bit."

"Does it feel good?"

"Yeah."

"Are you caressing it through your briefs?"

"Yeah."

"Good—remember what you're feeling, and later compare it with what you feel when you remove your briefs."

"Uh-huh. Should I take off my briefs now?"

"No, not yet. Wait a little while. Start stroking your dick."

"I am."

"Are you still caressing your crack?"

"I can't—I'll drop the phone."

"My love, last time you could. Try to do it."

"Let's see...done."

"Now put your hand under your briefs and touch your dick."

"Yeah."

"Tell me how you feel."

"I feel wonderful. I'm really hard. I'm rubbing my balls, too. You?"

"I'm stroking myself also, my love."

"And what're you stroking? How do you feel?"

"I'm rubbing my cock. I'm really hard just thinking about what you're doing...all right my love, now take off your briefs."

"Hold on."

"Rub your crack."

"Yeah."

"Does it feel even better without your briefs?"

"Sure does."

"Stick your finger up your ass."

"Uh-huh."

"But tell me what you're doing."

"O.K. I'm sticking a finger up my ass."

"Does it feel good?"

"Yeah. It hurts a little, but I like it."

"Why don't you use a little lubricant?"

"All right. Hold on... I'm putting some on now. I'm sticking part of my finger up my ass. I feel really great. I'd like for you to fuck me...for you to fuck me with your cock."

"Wait a minute, my love. Let's keep playing. Tell me how you feel."

"I feel really great—I already told you. I can feel how my finger is going further up into my ass. Now I have the whole finger inside."

"Oh, what a sweet boy, my love. Do you like it?"

"Yeah, yeah I really like it."

"How do you feel?"

"I feel excellent. I feel turned-on. My ass is hot. Now I'm pulling out my finger a little, and now I'm sticking it back in."

"Oh, my love, how delicious! Imagine I'm tonguing your ass, that I'm licking you, that I'm tonguing your hole...that I'm sticking my tongue way up your luscious ass."

"Uh-huh."

"Does it feel good?"

"Yeah."

"Put some more lubricant on."

"What for? There's no friction."

"Fine, but put just a little bit more on. Do it for me."

"O.K."

"All done?"

"Yeah. Now what?"

"Stick another finger up your ass."

"Two?"

"Yes."

"It's going to hurt."

"I don't think it's going to hurt, my love—you've endured bigger things."

"All right, let's see then... Oh, it feels so good."

"You're a little glutton. You really like taking it from behind, don't you?"

"Yeah, I really do. I'm sticking my fingers in even farther."

"Is your cock rock hard?"

"Yeah."

"Stroke it."

"All right... Hold on—I'm going to change positions. In the meantime, tell me what you're doing."

"Well, I'm stroking my cock also, my love. It's rock hard just thinking about your hot ass cheeks, so big, so shapely. And your fingers inside your ass. Oh, my love, how wonderful—I really want to eat you up from head to toe, all right?"

"Yeah, sure."

"What position are you in now?"

"Lying down—that way I can hold the phone better."

"Face up or face down?"

"Face up."

"Put your fingers in your ass again."

"I haven't taken them out."

"You changed position with your fingers still up your ass?"

"Yeah."

"You always want to have something up your ass, don't you, you little fucker?"

"Yeah."

"Not for one moment do you not want to have something up your ass."

"I'm stroking my cock now, too."

"Oh, how great. So am I—I'm stroking my cock also."

"Now I'm spreading my legs so I can get my fingers up my ass more easily."

"Oh, what a little fag you are, my love; how great. Do you like it?"

"Yeah, a lot...now I'm beating off."

"Tell me what you see, my love—while you're lying down."

"I see my rock hard cock. My hair. A part of my balls. I'm pushing up, then pulling down the foreskin. Now the head of my cock is exposed."

"Which do you like more—the feeling in your cock or in your ass?"

"Both—I like to feel both things at the same time."

"How great, my love. I really like trying to imagine how you're sticking your fingers up your ass."

"Oh, I want to come."

"Come whenever you want, my love."

"You too, shoot."

"Yes, my love; me too."

"I'm about to come."

"Stick your fingers in a little deeper."

"Oh, yeah, hmm... Oh, I'm going to come—you come too."

"Yeah, my love; come, come, shoot it all out."

"Oh..."

"Oh, my love, how great this is... Oh, I'm coming..."

"Did you come?"

"Yeah... Oh, I shot a huge load, my love. You?"

"Me too. I shot all the way to my neck."

"You were really hot, weren't you, you little fucker?"

"Sure was, and you?"

"Me too."

"You weren't feeling down today, were you?"

"No, no... I really like to fuck you, my love."

"Me too."

"This time I'm not going to fall into your trap—I already know what you're going to say: you too like to fuck yourself."

"That's right."

"And with me, right?"

"That too, man."

"Well, hang up if you want; I'm going to come in, all right?"

"O.K."

"..."

"..."

"Give me a kiss, my love."

"..."

"Let's see, let me help you. You want me to bring you a towel?"

"Sure."

"Do you want something to drink?"

"A Coke."

"Wouldn't you prefer some tea?"

"Oh, Santiago, if I'm telling you I want a Coke it's because I prefer a Coke. If not, I would tell you I want some tea."

"All right, my love. Tell Genaro to bring you a Coke and me some tea."

"O.K.... Genaro? Bring up a Coke for me and some tea for Santiago... No, in mine... O.K."

"My love, you didn't even say, 'please.' Come on."

"It's his job, isn't it? That's why you pay him. If he were a friend, I would have certainly said, 'please'."

"Well all right, but just because I pay him a salary is no reason to treat him badly."

"I didn't treat him badly, did I? I only told him what I wanted."

"Yes, Arturo, but... You have to treat the help staff with respect; if not... Well, if you expect others to treat you well, you have to begin by treating them well."

"Oh come on—you aren't really very happy with them either."

"You're right—I'm not pleased with them right at this moment, my love, but that's not why I'm going to... Look, it would be better for you to forget what I told you the other day—I wouldn't want to accuse anyone unjustly either."

"The same thing happened to my mother once."

"Yes, I can just imagine—Sarita also has a lot of valuable things. So what did she do?"

"Well, it wasn't anything very valuable—it was perfume. What she did was to go through one of the housemaid's things— the one she was suspicious of, but she never found anything. She fired her anyway without paying her her salary."

"Well deserved."

"Why, if she wasn't able to prove anything? My mother

threatened to tell the authorities because there were some other things missing. The young woman left crying and swearing she hadn't stolen anything."

"I'm sure she was using her tears to try to make Sarita feel bad. These people are capable of anything."

"But later the perfume turned up—which is to say—she didn't steal it."

"I'm sure she left it behind before she took off."

"No, it turned up a few months later."

"She probably told one of the other servants to return it, don't you think? They're all in cahoots—they all cover for one another. Maybe she had a guilty conscience, or she was afraid Sarita would carry out her threats."

"Who knows? I don't think it was her."

"Well, this experience was worthwhile for her even if she wasn't guilty. It will teach her to be more honest—if not for a real sense of conviction then out of fear. If at some future time she considers robbing someone, I can promise you she'll think twice before she does it... It's really unpleasant, isn't it? With these people there's nothing you can do, Arturo. Why are they like that? The more you give them, the more they want. Take my servants for example: I treat them well, I give them a huge salary...I mean they even have social security. And how do they repay me? By robbing me."

"Tell them to search really well, man."

"I already have, Arturo. Nothing. Look, it isn't so much the value of the things: when everything is said and done, what is that really worth? What bothers me is the fact that... I don't know; it seems to me it's a breach of trust. It's very unpleasant, don't you think? You just can't be going around all the time watching to see if they are going to rob you. And besides... Well, it's also no good to stop believing in people. If you put your trust in somebody, the minimum you can expect from that person is for him to perform at that level and to respond to your trust."

"Or threaten to fire them."

"No, I can't, Arturo. In the first place, because I don't know who it really was. I don't have any proof. And in the second place, don't think that's so easy to do here. I don't like to give them a reason to try to get back at me—you never know how they might react... Put something on, my love. Genaro will be here soon."

"Oh come on, he's not going to suspect anything."

"That's not the reason, my love. It's simply a question of setting yourself apart...of respect for oneself. You just can't allow a servant to see you undressed—that would create an intimacy for no reason whatsoever."

"O.K., O.K."

"I've really been preaching to you quite a bit lately, haven't I?"

"More or less."

"Forgive me, my love, but I'm doing it for your own good and to remind you of your social status."

"O.K."

"Did what I said bother you?"

"No."

"Really?"

"No, man, and stop asking me so many questions because then I will really get into a bad mood."

"Fine. Let's see...give me a kiss then... Who is my adorable hunk?"

"Well, I am—who else?"

"And who is my tasty little one?"

"Me."

"And my little companion?"

"Me."

"Well, put on your pants then."

"Oh, hold on a minute—I'm feeling so lazy."

"Put on your pants, my love, and if you want we can stay here all afternoon and rest."

"O.K."

"Do you want to watch television?"

"No."

"Do you want to take a nap?"

"No."

"Then what do you want to do?"

"Nothing. Tell me a story about something."

"What do you want me to tell you, my love? You already know everything about my life."

"Tell me about your first relationship."

"I've already told you about that, Arturo."

"You only told me it was really great, but I don't think that is all there is to it."

"What do you mean?"

"It's like when you talk about my mother—you say some things, but you hide others."

"What things do I hide?"

"What you don't like about her, or what you don't dare to see."

"Come on, my love—do you really think that?"

"Yeah. You always see just a part of something. I don't think everything was great in that relationship, was it?"

"No, of course not everything was great in that relationship. You're right, Arturo—at times I refuse to see certain things. I don't know why. Maybe it's due to—like a friend was telling me—the difficulty that I have dealing with pain. Or perhaps it's a more healthy attitude: the desire to not worry so much about small details and to not harbor resentment. I don't know. Well, yes... That relationship made me very happy, but it also caused a lot of headaches. No, not really headaches but a certain discomfort. Or maybe what happened was simply things turned out differently than what I was expecting... The first time that we had...um...we made love, there was some guilt attached. I mean, well, there was guilt, but there was also pride. Do you think those two feelings can coexist?"

"I don't know."

"That first time he possessed me I felt both things. On one hand, I felt proud...happy about finally having had my first relationship. I felt more complete as a human being. I don't know if I'm explaining this to you very well. Yes, I felt proud of having acquiesced to his request, of having conquered my fears. Maybe it's not that I felt more complete as a human being, but more...more in line with myself if you will. More in line with my desires, with my way of being, and that gave me a profound satisfaction, but at the same time, I felt...um...that I was completely used."

"What do you mean by that?"

"Well, hurt, humiliated. I felt humiliated."

"Because he got to fuck you first?"

"Maybe... No, it wasn't because of that. It was perhaps a guilty feeling for having gotten so intimate with someone. I don't know. It's hard to expose yourself completely to others. It leaves you with a strange feeling, as if you regret having done something, or...I don't know. I guess prostitutes must feel something similar when they charge for the first time."

"Do you think everyone feels like that the first time they fuck?"

"I don't know. Why don't you tell me—did you feel that way the first time we made love?"

"No."

"Maybe what's happening is that times have changed.

Now no one is shocked by anything. Now...but I don't think this feeling I'm talking to you about only has to do with sex. It also happens to you when you tell a friend something very intimate, like when you tell someone something you had never dared to say to anyone, something maybe you've never dared to tell yourself. Have you ever noticed when someone tells you something very intimate, later they feel embarrassed and shy away from you?"

"Yeah."

"It could take years for that friend to look you up again. Well, I think it's because of that contradictory feeling that I'm telling you. It's as if you thought: 'Damn, I shouldn't have told him anything, but it's great I dared to say it.' Do you understand what I'm saying?"

"Uh-huh."

"Curious, isn't it? Who knows the psychological term for that feeling? It must have a name. Well, that's how I felt... That night I couldn't sleep. I tossed and turned all night long. I'd feel all right and very happy for a little while, and then that kind of guilt would take over and... I'd get up and go to the bathroom and try to go back to sleep. I spent a very restless night. I spent the whole time thinking about the consequences of what I had done—not just the bad consequences but also the good ones. I was sure that act had changed my life forever."

"And did it?"

"Yes, of course, naturally... Suddenly I got sleepy and tried to fall asleep, but I just couldn't. I was in that midway stage between being awake and being asleep, that really strange stage like when you have a fever. It's like a kind of delirium, of...a state where you're not asleep or awake. Then I started to kind of hallucinate. Listen to how strange it was—in that state I felt as if my body were that of a man and of a woman at the same time...like with what I had done the differences between the sexes had been erased...the physical differences. Now I think that was due in part to being extremely tired—I was exhausted from not being able to sleep—but also in part because I hadn't been able to understand fully what had just happened."

"And him?"

"What about him?"

"What was he doing?"

"No, well, he was sleeping. He had already fallen asleep...I mean, for him it was all perfectly normal, right? I think he was around thirty years older than me. He no longer...he no longer was worried about this kind of thing. I don't even think it occurred to him I was having a really difficult time... Well, I mean, that state of confusion lasted for quite a while. I felt queer..."

"Well, that's because you were queer."

"Don't make fun of me, Arturo. Everything seems so normal to you because you grew up in a different time. I'd like to have seen you in my place. Don't think it was so easy to begin to accept myself, to... For me to be able to accept myself and to value myself—a lot of time had to pass. Back then it wasn't so easy...and that strange sensation lasted a long time. I felt really bad for a long time. I still see that part of my life as foggy. I felt so confused, so...you wouldn't believe it, Arturo, but it took me a lot of work and a long time to be able to...to feel comfortable with myself again."

"But did you continue to see him?"

"No, no. After that first encounter, he had to return to his place of origin."

"Oh come on, 'his place of origin': how mysterious!"

"Well, it wouldn't matter if it were Monterrey or Miami, would it? The thing is we didn't see each other for several years. The relationship started up again after about three years."

"And during that time, you didn't see him at all?"

"Not at all."

"But he'd call or write you."

"No, not that either. During that period of time, I practically didn't hear anything about him. I only found out about something once in a while when I'd hear my parents talking about him."

"Your parents?"

"He was a friend of the family. Didn't I mention this?"

"No, I don't think so."

"Well, he was a friend of theirs. I met him through my parents because he used to come over a lot and...and because of my parents, I continued finding out what he was doing. But beyond that, nothing. Now, on the other hand, I think it was best that way—maybe I would have felt bad if I had kept on seeing him... That time helped me to grow up and to mature a little bit. And that's about it...when we started seeing each other again, we managed to pick up the relationship but in a different way... Yes?... Come in... Thank you, Genaro... Take this away, please..."

"..."

"..."

"Keep going."

"What was I saying?"

"That when you started seeing each other the relationship was different."

"Well, yes. It had become another kind of relationship—thanks to the fact I had matured a little. And yes, in that stage there were more good things than bad... It was a very happy, fulfilling period in my life. We had a very stable relationship for many years... Well, maybe there were some problems, some misunderstandings like in any relationship... Your needs don't coincide with those of someone else all the time. But in general it was a really nice period in my life. It doesn't bother you for me to talk to you about these things?"

"I'm the one who asked you to tell me about them. Why would they bother me?"

"Well...I don't know...maybe out of jealousy."

"You already know I'm not the jealous type, Santiago. Go on."

"Well, there's not much more to add. You know how the saying goes—well, it's not a saying, it's a...you know what they say, that true love doesn't leave tracks. I wonder why we're like that."

"Who?"

"Everyone. Human kind in general. It seems we are pleased with pain and suffering. Those are the only things we can talk about—or those are the only things we like to talk about."

"Not me."

"Take Sarita for example. You yourself have observed when she has problems she's capable of spending hours on the phone."

"But also when she doesn't have problems. She's only capable of speaking quickly when she's the one who has to pay for the call."

"No, that's not true. The thing is... Well, maybe we have to talk about the bad stuff to put it behind us, to...to get rid of it because it's harmful to hang on to it. You already know what happens to someone who has a secret he can't tell: the secret ends up consuming him."

"What movie are you talking about?"

"No, I'm not talking about any movie—I'm talking about real life."

"Well, you have a funny way of saying it."

"But seriously, Arturo—what you can't confess is what hurts you the most. That's why there are so many psychoanalysts: that's how they make a living—from everyone else's secrets—that's how they get rich and make a fortune."

"Have you ever undergone psychoanalysis?"

"Only for a short time—just a few sessions."

"And did they help?"

"Well, yes, I think so, but that doesn't keep me from seeing the down side—we need a psychoanalyst because we have lost the ability to trust each other."

"And did you go back to him?"

"To the psychoanalyst?"

"No, to the mysterious man who was your lover."

"He's not a mysterious man, Arturo—don't make fun... No, I haven't seen him again. He passed away quite a while ago."

"What did he die of?"

"From an ulcer that ruptured, a... It was horrible. His death really affected me... Not just because he was someone with whom I had shared part of my life but because from that moment on I began to be aware of death. It's very difficult, don't think that... Every time someone close to you dies it's as if you die a little bit also... A part of your life dies... it's hard...you feel more and more alone. There comes a time when you receive an overwhelming amount of news about something like this, and ...the more you tell yourself things to console yourself...the more effort you make to meet new friends...you're more and more alone... Well, I'm sure talking a lot and about sad things. Why don't you tell me something?"

"Oh, no, I'm telling you I feel so completely lazy. You just keep talking. How long did your relationship last?"

"Several years—ten or twelve."

"What do you mean ten or twelve? Don't you remember?"

"Yes, of course, I remember. It's just that... Well, we lived together for ten years, and then... We kept the relation going for two more years, but we lived apart."

"Why?"

"Well, because... Well, I was really restless. That was

normal, right? I was younger and..."

"Younger?"

"Well, I was young, and uh, and...well, I felt like...like seeing the world, like..."

"Like fucking other people?"

"Well, yes, in a way. I had lived faithfully with him for several years, and it was normal, wasn't it, for me to want to...see the world? Up until that point in time, the only thing I knew about was his world: his friends, his get-togethers, his interests. We shared everything. I didn't have my own personality. I didn't have an identity. Of course, I realized this later on, but...look, when I was with him, almost everyone I ever came in contact with was twenty or thirty years older than me. I didn't have any friends my age."

"Just a bunch of old people."

"Yes, exactly. Well, I had some acquaintances like my classmates, but as far as friends I had made myself, no. My world was limited to just his."

"And my mother?"

"Well, I knew Sarita, but I didn't really see her very much at that time. We belonged to different groups. We only became good friends when my relationship ended. At that time Sarita had already married your father, and you were about to be born, but in spite of that, she continued to be very independent—you already know she's always been very jealous of her freedom, very..."

"So what did you do?"

"Do you mean when my relationship ended?"

"Yeah, did you take a trip, or what?"

"No, I didn't take a trip. I had already traveled a lot with my...with my friend. I wasn't talking about that when I said I needed to see the world. I was talking about the need to meet other types of people and to have other types of experiences... I began to live by myself. For the first time in my life I lived by myself."

"How old were you?"

"Thirty-two."

"You were already all grown up."

"Well, yes, physically I was all grown up as you say, but emotionally and psychologically I was like an adolescent who had just left his parent's house—I was very insecure; I ..."

"The good thing is you left."

"You're making fun of me, aren't you?"

"No, why would you say that? Keep going."

"Well, I was telling you I was really very insecure—super insecure. I felt completely confused. Realize I didn't know who I was—I had spent ten years with one person...with someone who had been a very strong point of reference, right? I had adopted his customs, his viewpoints, his... I had completely forgotten about myself in order to live like...like a couple. I turned out not knowing who I was, what I needed, or what I wanted. That's when, like I was telling you, I began to live by myself. And yes, at first it was extremely difficult—don't think it wasn't. It was almost like beginning again from square one...and, of course, I missed him a lot, but...my desire to know myself was stronger...and...well, I started meeting new people, making new circles of friends..."

"Were you working?"

"Yes, I worked ever since I graduated."

"But you didn't need to, did you?"

"No, I was not experiencing economic need, but yes... Let's just say I was working because of ... It wasn't because I needed money—it was a different kind of need. Financially I was independent, but in other ways I was not. That's when, like I was saying, I began to value myself, to..."

"And that's when you became a really good friend of my mother's."

"Yes."

"And she became your, how did you call it, your 'point of reference'?"

"Well, I had never thought about it like that..."

"You stopped imitating that other guy to start imitating her."

"Listen, who do you think you're talking to?"

"Well, you yourself said you learned a lot of things from her."

"Yes, of course, but...from the way you're talking it seems like you see me as a puppet, like a man without any will, without his own personality... Yes, Sarita was a decisive influence on my life, if you will, but not in the way you're insinuating. It was a very enriching friendship, very... Sarita gave me many things, but I'm sure I also gave her things as well. That's what friendship is like, isn't it? True friendship is a give and take—you give and you receive. Any other way, it's only a relation...um...a parasitic relationship in which you only try to see what you can get out of the other person... Well, Sarita and I were absolute best friends for a long time. We trusted each other completely; we had a lot of fun together, and when she became a widow, it was only natural for our friendship to become even stronger. We were practically inseparable. We went out a lot together; do you remember?"

"More or less."

"Don't you recall we would go to the house in the Valle de Bravo[11] neighborhood a lot?"

"I remember, but not very well. Other people went also, didn't they?"

"Yes, exactly, at times some of our other friends would go also. But...the bottom line was that Sarita and I were very lonely—she because of being a widow, and me because of my...well, I hadn't had another stable relationship. And later, well, I went through a profound crisis. A strange feeling came over me...I felt like I had lost my sense of values, that nothing made any sense. I began to feel very strange—as if I couldn't recognize myself in what I was thinking or feeling or even saying."

"Like when you had your first relationship?"

"Yes. Well, no; they were two distinct times even though... Well, what they had in common was that they were both crisis moments. I started to be afraid of everything...the most innocuous situations seemed threatening to me, and... I got sick a lot; I lost my appetite and my will to live."

"And all this happened to you when my father died?"

"No, I'm just saying..."

"How strange, Santiago—maybe you were in love with him."

"Oh come on—how can you even say that? This feeling didn't overtake me because your father died...it just happened when I was at an age when these types of crises are common. It's...well, it's when you realize you're no longer a boy and...that life in many ways is not what you were expecting. Well, maybe the death of your dad did affect me, but only indirectly. Perhaps it made me more aware of death, or... How strange—I've never really thought about it, but there could be something to that... And you can guess who was the only person at my side the whole time this crisis lasted."

"My mother."

"Yes. She went with me to the doctor; she took care of me; she cried with me. How can I not be grateful to her? Tell me that's not generous. If that's not generosity, I don't know what is."

"So why did you stop seeing each other?"

"Sarita has never told you?"

"No. Well, I never thought to ask her either."

"Well, we stopped seeing each other because of a... I was going to say it was because of a misunderstanding, but that's not the case—a misunderstanding would be what it's called if things had made it to the very end. No. Sarita and I stopped seeing each other because... Well, we were disgusted with each other; it was she who got angry with me because... Look, since we were feeling so lonely and...and since we saw how well we got along, one day we decided to get married."

"Really? So what were you going to do when..."

"It's really not necessary to be so obvious, Arturo. I know what you're referring to."

"So what were you going to do about it?"

"Don't think we hadn't talked about that aspect of our relationship—Sarita knew very well who I was. Nobody was fooling anyone. I'm telling you we had no secrets, Arturo, and that she accepted me completely."

"Then why were you going to get married?"

"Well, to be honest, don't think I was completely convinced about the whole thing. In fact, I brought up some delicate matters, especially: how were we going to deal with our...with her sexual needs? But it didn't seem to matter to Sarita."

"Because she had already bought a dildo to satisfy..."

"Don't be so ridiculous."

"I mean something to satisfy her, not you."

"Sex isn't the only thing that matters, Arturo."

"Especially if you're trying to get to something else, right? It seems to me my mother was after your money."

"Oh, Arturo, as soon as the topic of your mother comes up, you make everything so ugly. It appears you can't see her without becoming emotional. Try to be fair...and stop interrupting me if you want to know why we ended our friendship—temporarily, of course."

"Sure, so tell me."

"Well, in spite of that, of those kinds of inconveniences—
if that's what you want to call them—we decided to get
married. What we needed was someone at our side—a
more constant and stronger support. We both needed a
lot of affection, and that's something we could certainly
give one another...well, we set a date for the wedding
and...we were only going to have the civil ceremony; don't
think for a moment we were going to go through all the
fuss of a religious ceremony, and...well, in the beginning it
seemed like a good idea. But later as the date we had
decided on drew near, I began to realize, instead of feeling
calmer, the situation was making me very anxious. I began
to feel bad again—very distressed, very... I felt in my heart
instead of making things better, marriage was only going to
make them worse, to complicate them even more. And I
began to think seriously about the possibility of not marrying
Sarita. Of course the more time passed, the harder it was
to get out of the situation, right? and the more anxious I
felt...but I decided once again to be completely honest with
myself, and with my heart in pieces as they commonly say,
I decided to confront Sarita and tell her no."

"So what did she do?"

"Well, at first she tried to persuade me otherwise, but
later, after realizing I wasn't giving in, she became furious.
You can't imagine. She insulted me, she... Well, she even
told me what I was going to die of. She...she tried to hit
me; she slapped me; she said really horrible things to me—
things I didn't think she was capable of saying."

"Like what?"

"Oh, I really don't remember, Arturo. Really hurtful
things that mostly had to do with my sexual orientation.
Um...I don't know; it was really ugly—she took advantage
of intimate things I had told her because I trusted her a lot,
and she threw some things in my face that, well, even though
they were true, she didn't need to use them against me—

much less in public."

"What do you mean in public? Where were you?"

"In a café. We had gone to have a coffee and to talk and...perhaps it was not one of my better ideas, but I decided I was going to tell her about my decision there. That's when she started acting like a lunatic and began screaming insults at me right there in front of everyone. Oh, it was a very awkward situation and very...very unexpected because I didn't think Sarita was capable of making such a scene."

"You're so naïve—she's capable of that and much more."

"Yes, I believe that now, but I didn't at that time. I had another image of Sarita—an image of a very respectful, very liberal, and tolerant person, but...but I'm telling you her outbreak was extremely vulgar and ugly, and...and selfish... Oh, you can't imagine how embarrassing it was... It took me a long time to get over it, and a lot of years had to pass for... Sarita and I stopped seeing each other for a long time, but well, that's all in the past, isn't it? Fortunately. Now we're the best of friends again... So...well, everything is in the past as I was saying; we've forgiven each other because we both made mistakes, and... It's crazy, isn't it? The problems you can get yourself into when you don't know what it is you really want...or when you're in dire need of affection and you don't know the best way to go about getting it... Loneliness and sadness are bad advisors. I had always thought so, but my situation proved it. They make you do the most foolish things even to the point of losing your own dignity...but, well, that's life; what are you going to do? You don't always have aces in your hand. Don't think for a moment that once in a while I don't stop myself and think... Well, there are moments when I ask myself if maybe I made the wrong decision by not marrying her even though I was completely convinced I didn't want to...at times I stop and think if it would have been better the other way around... I don't know... Probably... Who knows how my life would have turned out if Sarita and I had decided to get married at that time?"

"You would have certainly gotten my ass a lot sooner."

"Hey! How can you say that? I may be very insecure, foolish—everything that you say I am, but I'm not without a conscience. You'd have to be really bold, really... No, no way. I suppose you're just joking—aren't you?"

"Maybe not. The only difference is you wouldn't have had to spend so much to get it."

"Oh, Arturo, at times you think and say anything! Of course I wouldn't have; I already told you—if I had married Sarita, everything would have been very different. I would have tried...well, to have been a father to you."

"Daddy!"

"Stop playing around like that, Arturo."

"And suppose you had wanted to fuck me, especially seeing me in shorts all over the house like you say?"

"That's not the case, Arturo—things didn't happen that way. Fortunately."

"But, come on, what would you have done?"

"Nothing. I would have held out—I would have tried to satisfy my desire some other way."

"Having me so close by?"

"Yes, having you so close by. Sex isn't everything, Arturo. Maybe you think it is because you're at an age when that need is very strong, but it's not everything. There are other important things, other... If I had married Sarita, I would have had other responsibilities, and rest assured I would have fulfilled them... What? Are you going to watch television?"

"I just want to see what's on."

"There's nothing on now, my love. The good shows come on at night."

"Hold on."

"It's better if we continue the conversation."

"Oh, no. I'm bored now. We always end up talking about the same thing."

"About what?"

"About my mother."

"Oh, my love, if we were talking about her, it's because you wanted to."

"Me?"

"You asked me why we had stopped seeing each other, didn't you?"

"Maybe, but I'm bored with that now."

"All right, my love—you're the king here and everywhere. Your wish is my command."

"Don't get carried away."

"You know it's true, my love."

"Speaking of wants, I'm going to need more money, Santiago… I'm short of money and want to buy some clothes."

"Oh, my love, I just gave you some."

"Don't be stingy, man. It's all right if you want to be like my mother, but don't be like her in this."

"You think I'm stingy?"

"Show me you're not."

"Up until right now, I have never denied you anything, Arturo."

"Then don't start."

"No, no, but… What did you do with what I gave you?"

"I bought a few things."

"What things?"

"Are you asking me to justify my behavior? You told me you weren't going to ask me to justify my behavior when we lived here."

"No, my love—I'm not asking you to justify your behavior."

"If you want, I'll show you the receipts."

"No, my love—that's not necessary. You know you're free to do what you want, but..."

"But what?"

"It's just that I hope...you aren't misspending it...that you're not going to pick up a bad habit."

"It's only the vice of buying."

"As long as it's that vice, it's all right. It doesn't bother me to encourage that in you. But be careful with any other vice, Arturo. If you don't do it for yourself, do it for me, for this little old guy who loves you so; my love, just think, what receipts would I give to Sarita in case of...?"

"O.K., O.K., don't start preaching again. Are you going to give me the money, yes or no?"

"Yes, of course, my love. How much do you want?"

"Three hundred."

"Oh, Arturo, aren't you getting into a bad habit?"

"But you said it was all right, didn't you? As long as it was for buying things it wasn't a problem."

"No, my love—it's not a problem."

"Besides, you're going to come out ahead, too."

"Why? Are you going to buy me something?"

"Because I'm going to look even better. And the people who know you are going to say, 'Wow, what a hunk Santiago has,' don't you think?"

"Of course they are, my love. Then go ahead and buy something tight so your...hmmm...your delicious shapes can be admired...."

"I'll see what I can find. Give it to me then."

"Right this second?"

"Yeah."

"You're going to leave right this second?"

"Yeah. What's wrong with that?"

"Weren't you so tired?"

"Well, not anymore. We've been resting."

"Do you want me to go with you?"

"Whatever you'd like."

"No, it would be better if I stayed here—that way... You won't get mad if I stay here?"

"I already told you I don't care."

"While you're gone, I'll make some phone calls."

"You're going to call my mother again?"

"No, my love: Sarita is not my only friend."

"You always call her after we fuck. Why? Do you feel guilty?"

"No, Arturo. I'm not going to talk to her. I have other friends."

"Well, tell her 'hello' for me."

"But my love, I just told you..."

"I'm leaving, Santiago. Are you going to give me the money?"

"Yes, my love—wait just a second; I'll bring it to you right away."

DECEMBER

"Don't you want something else?"

"No."

"They make really delicious brownies here. Go ahead, have one."

"I don't want one. Why don't you get one?"

"No, I can't, my love—I'm already a little in the red."

"I have money if you need some. Or we can pay with plastic."

"Oh, my love—I'm not talking about that—I'm in the red with my calories. I'm over my limit with food."

"Well, have one, and tomorrow you can go on a diet."

"No, no. You have to know how to say no. It's a sign of maturity. At my age you can't have it all, Arturo; you can't have a decent shape and eat everything you want."

"Oh, now you're sounding like my mother."

"And like *many other* people my age, my love—not just Sarita. It's bad enough if you go a little overboard with the food, you ruin all the work it's taken to lose weight—or just to maintain. Don't think it's easy... When you're young, you can allow yourself to eat anything, Arturo. Your body works in a different way; your metabolism works well; your... After forty, or maybe before, things change radically—to make up for eating just a little bit of extra food, you have to diet for several days and increase your workout time quite a bit. Everything is more difficult—to get over a hangover sometimes takes you two or three days; an extra cup of coffee keeps you up all night; it takes longer to get over most illnesses. Well, without getting too carried away, just one sleepless night can leave you looking monstrous for several days..."

"Well there's a cure for that."

"Yes, I know, my love, but I'd like to take care of myself before going under the knife. I'd leave that as a last recourse."

"Why? Because you're so worried about what others might say about you?"

"No, no, it's not because of that, Arturo. It's more like... I think it's a question of sincerity, of honesty, or I don't know how to say it... Look, you can hide the passage of time, but you can't hide your age from yourself. It's no use to have your face all ironed out if your body is already full of aches and pains and you don't have any energy."

"Well, a lot of people say they feel great after they've been operated on."

"That may be true, but it's just a fleeting euphoria. You'll soon be at the mercy of the passing of years again, and it will be even worse. Naturally, I've seen many examples... Plus there's nothing more pathetic than the people who refuse to grow old. It's... Suddenly, you as a spectator, become annoyed to see the lengths to which someone will go to try to stay looking young. It's a battle lost before it even starts. They become ridiculous in their zeal to keep looking young."

"You were thinking about my mother, weren't you?"

"No, no, not at all, Arturo."

"Because she's like that—you can't deny it."

"Well, maybe there's something to that, but I wasn't thinking about her. Besides, Sarita is a woman, and that changes things. Women worry more about beauty and how they look, and that's natural—it's always been that way."

"Then who were you thinking about?"

"I was thinking about the friends we just visited. Take Roy—he's a perfect example of what I was saying. The poor guy no longer knows what to do to himself to keep others from noticing his age. They've operated on him who knows how many times; he's had liposuction, peelings—well, everything you can imagine. Think about what his face looks like now—he looks like a little old skull with bulging eyes. And if all that made his life more pleasant, it would be well worth it, right? But it's not like that; he has to be very careful about everything he does; he can't even sunbathe."

"What a drag."

"And his friend, Lalo, isn't too far behind—his insistence of wanting to look like a young man when he no longer is, isn't anything short of ridiculous."

"And pathetic."

"And pathetic—exactly."

"About how old are they?"

"Well, Roy must be around my age, and Lalo is a little younger, but don't think he's a lot younger... I don't know—you just can't tell with people like that. Who knows why they do it, but it's sad, isn't it? To have the same haircut you had when you were a young man and...to wear the same kinds of clothes—those tight T-shirts and... And also that desperate need, I'd say, of surrounding themselves with young men so as to revitalize themselves or... Whenever you go to their house—like this last time we were there—there are always three or four young men prowling around... Well, maybe 'prowling' isn't the right word—surely they were invited, don't you think? But it gives you the impression they have no business being there; they're not in Roy and Lalo's social class, nor are they... They're there to see what they can get out of Roy and Lalo; there's no real affinity among them..."

"And do you think Roy and Lalo fuck them?"

"I don't know. I've asked myself the same question—don't think I haven't."

"But they're not even all that good-looking."

"No, no, I'm telling you their only worth to Lalo and Roy is that they're young, and Lalo and Roy practice a sort of unchecked cult to youth...but, hey, we're being way too critical of them. After all, they're still very lovely people, don't you think?"

"I think they're nothing more than some old queens without any redeeming value. I don't know why you have anything to do with them."

"Well yes, I agree with you somewhat, Arturo. They're very conventional people, quite foolish, not very sophisticated if you will. They don't have any class at all; they have all the defects of new money... The business about showing us their photo albums seemed in very poor taste. They feel so honored because those artist wannabes—who are only known in Miami—visit them, or those has-been singers from Mexico who have to go abroad to make a living. And to top it off, to get their pictures taken with them and to go around boasting they are their friends—well, that's pitiful, isn't it? That really speaks to their low self-esteem, don't you think?"

"Just like my mother! She's also impressed by every asshole who comes along!"

"Excuse me, Arturo, but your mother surrounds herself with people who certainly are worthwhile, people who are doing things, people who..."

"But it's the same thing—she seeks them out only because of their name—their name is what matters to her. It doesn't matter if they're an asshole, or haven't you picked up on that? She always saying, 'So and So called me,' giving their complete name as if anyone cared someone famous spoke to her. And she'll tell you their complete name so you realize she's a friend of theirs. You haven't missed out on that, have you? Because if she uses just the first name, then the person isn't important, get it? It can be whoever. On the other hand, if she uses the last name, you know it's someone famous, and what's more it was he that called her. That way, she's the important one—the most important. Deep down, my mother is like a whore—

she's capable of anything as long as she's accepted. She always knows to tell someone what they need to hear even if it's unpleasant."

"Oh, my love, you're getting carried away. I don't know why you're so hostile toward your mother…and why you have so much resentment. It seems like a total contradiction—instead of missing her…instead of wanting to see her, the fact you're by yourself, so far away from her—only contributes to your animosity toward her."

"That's right—the less I see her, the more I hate her."

"Don't say that, please, Arturo—it's impossible for you to hate your mother."

"When I'm around her, I can more or less stand her, but as soon as I don't see her, I always remember her idiocies, her desire to want to impress, and her way of always wanting to seem superior."

"It's like an obsession, isn't it, my love, that just won't leave you alone… How terrible—poor Sarita…I wonder how much she harmed you without even realizing it."

"I feel like puking."

"Do you want me to stop, my love?"

"No, man—I'm just joking."

"Let's talk about something else; let's speak positively about someone."

"But who?"

"Whomever. About the friends we just visited for example. You can't deny, in spite of everything, in spite of all the defects you can name, they also have good qualities."

"Like what?"

"Well, one of them is they're kind, loving people, don't you think so?"

"I don't know."

"They smother you with attention; they know how to make

you feel good..."

"Well, maybe that's what you think, but I was bored to tears. They may be very nice, but they bore me—they only talk about stupid things."

"Oh, my love, and I'm the one who thought you'd really like our little getaway."

"Well, I didn't."

"You didn't even like the visit we made to the observatory? How interest..."

"Hardly. It would have been better if we had gone somewhere else—to New York for example."

"But, my love—we were just there. It's good to have a change of pace."

"We were there *two months* ago, Santiago—I had just gotten here."

"Well, we'll go again another time, Arturo."

"You said we were going to do a lot of traveling. You tricked me—we've hardly gone anywhere."

"Oh, my love—don't say that...that makes me feel bad."

"Well, then feel bad. I feel bad, too. I'm bored—I'm either at home or at school. And when we do go anywhere, we go to see those tired old queens...what a bunch of bullshit."

"But don't get mad, my love. I asked you if you wanted to spend the weekend with them, and you said yes."

"That's because I didn't know they were so boring and stupid."

"All right, my love; forgive me."

"..."

"What can I do so you'll forgive me?"

"This is why I moved here? To be confined and not see anything except your friends?"

"Well, you came to study, Arturo—don't forget. That

was the deal we made with your mom. And...besides, I want to think you're here with me because you want to be here, because our relationship matters to you."

"But you said we were going to travel a lot."

"Arturo, we can't spend all of our time traveling—I have things to do here."

"You said we were going to have a lot of fun, and the only one having any fun is you—I'm certainly not."

"All right—forgive me."

"..."

"Oh, my love—don't be like that."

"Let's get out of here."

"You don't want anything else?"

"I already told you I didn't."

"Then let's go. Do you want to drive?"

"No."

"Bundle up, Arturo."

"..."

"You're not going to forgive me?"

"..."

"Oh come on, will you? What can I do so you'll forgive me?"

"I don't know."

"Do you want to take a trip?"

"Where?"

"Wherever you want to go, my love, but please get rid of that gloomy expression on your face... Where do you want to go?"

"I don't know."

"Wouldn't you like to go to Europe?"

"I've already been to Europe."

"Oh, my love; you don't go to places just so you can say you've been there—you go because you had a good time there."

"..."

"Or maybe you want to go to some exotic place with beaches and everything?"

"I don't know."

"Remember in the southern hemisphere summer is about to begin."

"..."

"You knew that, didn't you?"

"What?"

"That when it's winter here, it's summer there, and vice versa."

"Why is that?"

"Well, because... Well, because that's the way it is—right now we are farther from the sun, and they're closer. That's why it's cold here and hot there."

"Oh. Then they put up their Christmas tree when it's really hot?"

"Yes, of course."

"Well, that's ridiculous. And do they drink punch and roast chestnuts?"

"I guess they do. Wouldn't you like to find out for yourself?"

"I couldn't care less, Santiago[12]."

"Well, where would you like to go then, my love?"

"Anyplace, man. The thing is to get out of here."

"Well, don't say another word— we'll go to the travel agency tomorrow to make reservations."

"But where are we going?"

"What do you think about leaving it to chance? We can decide when we're at the agency."

"O.K. And you're going to buy me everything I want?"

"Of course, my love—have I ever denied you anything? What's more, you'll have your own travelers checks so you can buy whatever you want. Does that seem all right?"

"O.K."

"..."

"..."

"This is sure a great highway, isn't it?"

"More or less."

"You really feel like you're in a civilized country here, don't you? It's even a pleasure to drive—no holes, no animals, no trash. You just sail along without even noticing. These lovely highways are like your skin, my love, smooth, without anything that...like you...you're totally smooth...I can caress you without my hand finding obstacles in its way. Mmmm, how tasty... Well, the bottom line is things work, right? That's where you find out how developed a country is—in its order, its cleanliness, in its...in the fact things are made of the highest quality and everything, starting with food, is first class. Well, it goes without saying it's first world."

"..."

"Are you still mad?"

"I wasn't mad, Santiago. I told you I was bored...fed up."

"But not of me, right?"

"No. I told you I was fed up with feeling like I was always trapped inside."

"All right, my love, but we already took care of that. We agreed we were going to take a trip, didn't we?"

"Uh-huh."

"..."

"..."

"Well, the year is already over, isn't it? Time really flew, didn't it?"

"Uh-huh."

"And what are your resolutions for the new year?"

"I don't have any."

"Why don't you say, 'To love you more, Santiago'?"

"Why? You don't think I love you?"

"Yes, yes, my love—sure I do. It was just a joke. I know you love me a great deal. Thank you, my love. Thank you for giving me this total happiness at my age."

"Oh, don't start up again about your age. It's like you don't have anything else to talk about."

"Does it bother you I talk about it?"

"It bores me. Just like you said my hatred for my mother is an obsession, age is an obsession for you."

"But..."

"You only say it so people will tell you that you look good, that you look really good for someone your age. You always want people to tell you that."

"Why do you say 'people?' I only care what you think."

"Well, it sure doesn't seem like it. You talk about that with everyone. You think I'm not bored with listening to you and your friends talking about age all the time? That you're already so old, that you're so...I don't know...that life isn't the same any more. It's such bullshit—you don't have anything else to talk about."

"Listen—that's not true. I don't talk about that with all of my friends—with Roy and Lalo for example..."

"With those old queens you don't talk about your ages because they refuse to accept they're already old. But it's the same anyway—they don't talk about their age, but everything they do has to do with their age—should they get an operation, should they go around with younger men, should they...I don't know what."

"That's true, isn't it? That topic is always present even

though it's not directly mentioned. That's really in poor taste."

"It bores me to death, but I think it bothers you. Do you know why it bothers you?"

"No, my love—tell me."

"It bothers you because you're always thinking you're old even though you say it in jest. Then, the older you feel, the more you talk about it. It's a vicious cycle, like you're fond of saying."

"You're right, my love. I promise you I'm going to make an effort to not talk about that, O.K.?"

"O.K."

"Let's talk about something else then... Let's see, if you had to make a balance sheet of how last year was for you, what would you say?"

"Oh, I don't know, Santiago—I'm not a business person; I don't know anything about balance sheets."

"It's just a way of speaking in a figurative sense. At times I get the impression you just shut yourself off from the world."

"Not even if I were a clam."

"You see, Arturo? That's what I'm trying to tell you. You always make fun of the way I talk. And when you do that, the conversation doesn't go anywhere."

"Well, what do you want to know?"

"Well, just that, exactly what I was asking you—if you had to make a ...let's call it an evaluation of what the past year meant to you, what would be some of the more memorable things?"

"The most important?"

"Yes."

"That I got away from home."

"..."

"..."

"Nothing else?"

"Well, that I've traveled. A little, but at least I've traveled."

"What else?"

"Well, that's the most important."

"And the fact you're studying...that doesn't matter to you?"

"Yeah, but..."

"Or your relationship with me?"

"That too. But the most important thing is I got to leave my house because I just couldn't stand to be there any more."

"Do you value my company, my love?"

"Uh-huh."

"And what I do for you?"

"That too, man."

"How nice for you to say it."

"And what was the most important thing for you?"

"What I value most is to be with you."

"And besides that?"

"I also feel I've had other kinds of successes."

"Like what?"

"I made some good business deals, some investments that...that go beyond my expectations."

"You made a lot of money?"

"Let's just say I made enough to continue enjoying a certain sense of security... Something else I really value was rekindling my friendship with Sarita."

"Just don't tell me it was very important for you and you're so thankful to her."

"No, my love—you already know that."

"But you always say that to me."

"All right...I won't mention it anymore."

"So what else?"

"I also value the fact I'm well, that I have good health, that...well, why not say it? That I'm still attractive. Those are things...for which I should be thankful—not everyone has them. But above all that, I already told you what I value most, Arturo: your company, your love your... I adore you, my love—I'm really fond of you—you look so handsome."

"I look handsome or I am handsome?"

"Well, you are handsome, but today you look especially handsome."

"Why?"

"I don't know. Maybe it's...well, maybe I like to see you angry."

"Don't be silly. Why?"

"Because you seem like a temperamental child. At times you use some gestures that are kind of childish, which I really enjoy—when you make your mouth like that for example."

"Me?"

"Yes. It's understandable at times you act like a child—after all, you are very young, and age-wise you're still close to being just a boy."

"Oh."

"But I find the contrast fascinating—on one hand your childish gestures, your pouting, your tantrums, and on the other hand, there's your developed, muscular, delectable body. All of a sudden, I think I'm with a semi-perverse child, who besides playing, likes to get fucked. Oh, that's such a turn-on for me, my love...just thinking about your luscious ass makes my mouth water. I'm ready to gobble it up! Oh, I'd really like to do all kinds of dirty stuff with you right this minute."

"Here? In the car?"

"Yes, I'd really enjoy it."

"And where are you going to park?"

"Let's see if we can't find someplace a little bit up the road."

"Oh, no."

"I'd love to bite your ass cheeks...hmmm! And then rub my tongue along your crack and eat your ass—that would really turn me on. I'd eat it, and I'd put my tongue in your hot ass as far as I could until you said, 'Oh, I can't stand it any longer, please fuck me—stick it in all the way.' And then I'd give it to you and make you come just from the pure pleasure I was giving you with my dick. That is so hot...I'm getting so hard; look at what my cock is like... What are you laughing at?"

"Nothing."

"Oh, my love—don't make fun of the desire you awaken in me."

"I'm not making fun of that. I'm laughing about something else."

"What?"

"I was just trying to imagine the position in which you were going to eat my ass."

"And how were you imagining it?"

"Well, since there isn't any room, I'd have to stick half of my body out of the window, and who knows what the people passing by would think?"

"Yes, that would be amusing, wouldn't it?... I'm really hot—here, feel my dick so you can see how hard I am."

"..."

"Don't you want to?"

"Not right now."

"Why not?"

"Oh, because it's not very comfortable."

"It wouldn't be the first time you did it in a car, would it, you little fucker?"

"I've *never* done it in a car, Santiago, but *I'd guess* it would be really uncomfortable."

"Well, it also has its own thrill—the allure of something prohibited, the feeling someone could surprise you, that a patrol unit would show up unexpectedly..."

"Well, I'm not into it."

"So what are you saying? You don't want me to stop?"

"I just told you I didn't, Santiago—don't be insistent."

"Oh, my love."

"..."

"...Well, at least give me a blow job. Look at what you've done to me—my cock is rock hard and wants to unload...it's even beginning to hurt from being so hard. Go ahead, all right?

Give me a quick blow job."

"No."

"Why not?"

"Because I don't want to, Santiago—I just told you. I don't feel like it. I'm tired."

"Of what, my love? You rested all weekend long."

"Your friends wore me out—you don't think it's tiring to have to listen to their idiotic babbling all day long?"

"Go ahead, all right?"

"I won't."

"Just one quick suck. Look at how hard I am. I might damage myself if I can't get any relief."

"..."

"Just one quick little suck?"

"Oh, Santiago."

"Go ahead, my love."

"O.K., but what are you going to give me?"

"Oh, my love—what do you mean what am I going to give you? I give you everything you want—besides, everything that's mine is yours."

"Yeah, but what are you going to give me right now?"

"Oh, Arturo, you're really confusing me. It seems you want me to pay you for this."

"I'm going to say it like you do, 'Well, I wouldn't say it that way'."

"Then how?"

"I would say if I'm going to do something I don't want to do, it would be good for me to get something in exchange."

"All right. What do you want me to give you?"

"Um...A leather jacket."

"Well—count on it, all right?"

"O.K."

"Come on, help me, my love..."

"You're not going to stop?"

"No...Look how hard I am."

"Let's not have a wreck."

"Why would you say that, my love? I still have really good reflexes."

"..."

"Yeah, like that, my love...that feels great! Like that..."

"Are you sure you can still drive?"

"Yes, my love—keep going."

"Tell me when you're about to come, all right?, so I don't swallow your cum."

"Yes, sure."

"And you'll stop for a moment, won't you?"

"*Of course*, my love. Don't think I'm inconsiderate."

"Unconscious[13] is exactly how you'll be when you come—you'll see."

"I sure hope your hot little mouth knows what it's talking about."

"..."

"Oh, my love, what a good boy you are!"

Three

I

"There's nothing like being back home again!"

"Oh, Santiago, it seems you don't like to travel."

"Yes, of course I do, Arturo. I love to travel, especially with you. You don't know how much I enjoy it, but I also like being here at home, don't you?"

"More or less. I prefer to travel."

"Well, yes, traveling certainly has its appeal, but... If you want me to be honest with you, I was beginning to miss my own bed—I don't sleep as well anywhere else. Besides...well, your house is your place. Your anchor. It's always good to have a residence you can return to. It gives you a feeling of...well, of security, and that's very pleasant, isn't it? There's no place like home."

"When you say something like that you really come across as an old man."

"Maybe that's because I am."

"I thought you weren't going to talk about that any more."

"You're the one who brought it up, my love."

"But I was only getting you to hear yourself so you realize what you sound like."

"Well, thanks—I'll pay more attention to what I say."

"And when I said, 'old man,' I wasn't thinking about people your age—at your age, most people aren't like that. I was thinking of an eighty-year-old man."

"Oh, my love, I swear there are times when I feel that old."

"You see? You absolutely love to talk about age."

"No..."

"Now you're going to say, 'No, no, why do you say that? It's just that... Well, at times I get so tired and...'"

"Well, yes—you know me so well—I was going to say something like that. And it's true; don't think it isn't."

"Maybe it's true, but it seems to me a lot of your fatigue and your aches and pains and everything you say is psychological. I'm sure if you didn't talk about it so much, you'd feel better."

"Oh, Arturo, you're really surprising me. You say some very...very astute things to me, very pointed. You seem to have a very profound knowledge of human nature."

"Everything is so 'very'."

"Yes, everything is with 'very.' In that sense, you're...forgive me for saying this, but you're very similar to Sarita: both of you have a..."

"We had agreed we weren't going to talk about her anymore."

"Oh, my little dictator!"

"Let's make an agreement—from now on, you have to pay me twenty dollars every time you mention her, O.K.?"

"Oh, my love, that's really... It's all right you prohibit me from talking about age because it's bad for me, but to talk about Sarita, what harm can that cause?"

"Not to you, to me—you know I can't stand her."

"Your Christmas spirit certainly didn't last very long, Arturo!"

"My Christmas spirit lasted as long as I needed it to last— for Christmas Day. The name says it all: 'Christmas spirit,' right?"

"All right, let's not get into an argument over this also."

"I'm not arguing. I'm only clearing things up for you."

"All right then... Are you hungry?"

"A little. Are we going out for dinner?"

"Do you want to?"

"I'm just asking you if we're going out—I'm not saying I want to."

"But, do you?"

"I don't care."

"Why don't we stay in? I feel like eating something home made. Besides, I'm really tired."

"Then why did you ask me? We always end up doing what you want to do."

"Don't say that, please, Arturo—at least acknowledge my efforts to try to please you."

"All right, let's see...and if I had said I wanted to go out?"

"Then we would have gone out. That's why I asked."

"Even though you're tired?"

"Even though I'm tired. I would have made the effort for you."

"Well, yes, I want to go out."

"Really?"

"Yeah."

"All right. Let me take a quick shower and ..."

"Take two aspirins with a Coke. That's what my mother does when she's really tired and has to go out—or when she invites someone over. She claims that's a fool proof way to be chatty. I mean more chatty."

"Now *you're* the one talking about her."

"But it's not a taboo subject for me—the one who it's a taboo subject for is you."

"All right. I'm going to go get cleaned up."

"It's not true, man."

"What's not true?"

"That I want to go out for dinner."

"Are you serious?"

"Yeah."

"Oh, that's great good news, my love."

"I was just testing you."

"Did I pass the test?"

"Yeah. It was close, but you passed it."

"Well, I hope you remember this."

"O.K."

"So you really don't want to go out?"

"Oh, Santiago—I just told you I didn't."

"All right. Then I'm going to tell Chabela to fix us some soup. I love to have soup after returning from a long trip— it gives me the feeling I'm back home again."

2

"Look how nice!"

"Uh-huh."

"I didn't even remember this place anymore."

"Well, what a bad memory you have."

"Well, I mean yes I remember it but not in detail. It's really pretty. It's a shame the service wasn't very good."

"It's just as you say, 'Total bliss doesn't exist'—nor does scenery or service."

"Right!... Well, after all it wasn't so bad, was it?"

"That's where you had insomnia, isn't it?"

"Yes, that was horrible—do you remember I spent the whole night awake? The next day I couldn't even ... Well, yes, in fact, I look like a zombie—I can't stand that part of the video."

"But that scene *isn't* from the day you had insomnia."

"You see what you're like?... Do you know why I think I couldn't sleep that night, thinking about it now?"

"Why not?"

"Mosquito bites—I've never been bitten so much in my life."

"Oh, Santiago, there weren't any mosquitoes in the room."

"No, but they had bitten me before. I think they caused a slight allergic reaction."

"Don't make things up, man. You were probably worried about something."

"Not that I remember. In fact, I was feeling pretty good... Look how handsome you are there, my love."

"Just there?"

"No, you always look handsome, but you really look especially handsome in that scene. You're a real hunk."

"Really?"

"Yes—you look like a model from *Exercise*."

"Oh, Santiago, you and your comparisons."

"What about them?"

"Nothing, but at times they're terrible."

"Well, you look like one of the most handsome models from *Exercise*—the *most* handsome. Really—you're absolutely gorgeous. What an ass you have!"

"You should have filmed me nude."

"Oh, no, my love—suppose someone would have shown up? No, why would you want to risk that? Much less in a foreign country—that would have been the last straw. No... Besides, your bathing suit doesn't leave much to the imagination."

"What? You think it's kind of daring?"

"A little. Everyone was looking at you if you'll remember."

"But *not* because of the bathing suit."

"You're a bit vain, really, my love. Although I think you're right—when you have *so much* to be vain about, vanity isn't a defect—it's just a fair appreciation of what you're worth."

"You mean it?"

"Of course I mean it. If I didn't, I wouldn't be saying it. Oh, my love, you're such a hunk. Rewind that a little."

"What for?"

"To see you again. Mmmm! You don't know how much it turns me on to see you like that—almost nude in the water."

"Oh, Santiago—don't start."

"Why not, my love? What's wrong with that?"

"Let's stop watching it, man. You can watch that part as many times as you want by yourself."

"All right... Oh, look, I look terrible, and not just because of the insomnia."

"It's all right, man. You look halfway handsome."

"Really?"

"Uh-huh."

"Let's see—rewind it."

"..."

"Oh, no...how ugly—look at how my stomach muscles look—totally flabby. Do they really look like that?"

"That's because you're bending over. If you had stood up straight, you wouldn't have looked like that."

"You think so? Well, anyway, when we edit this, we'll take out this part. There are also some other parts that aren't very good. Look, in that scene I don't look so bad."

"Well, that's what I'm telling you—it's because you're standing up straight."

"Yes, you're right... I look like I should there and not like a ninety-year-old man."

"Oh, don't exaggerate."

"..."

"..."

"Do you really love me, my love?"

"You already know that I do."

"Even though I'm not young anymore?"

"Yeah, man."

"And even though my muscles look a little flabby at times?"

"Oh, yeah, man—that doesn't have anything to do with it."

"Why not?"

"Because it doesn't."

"But why not?"

"Because that's not the most important thing."

"Then what is the most important thing?"

"Other things, man."

"What things? My money?"

"Yeah."

"Oh, my love, you see what you're like? I wanted you to say something nice, and you end up telling me you're with me because of my money."

"I didn't say that, Santiago. You're the one who said it. I didn't even mention money."

"But you agreed—you said yes."

"But I said it just to make you mad. It really annoys me you're always thinking about that."

"Well, tell me what other things you really like about me *besides* my money."

"*Besides?* I didn't say I liked your money. I don't think about money, Santiago—or at least *not as much* as you think. The one who thinks about money is you."

"Listen, that's not..."

"I believe you have to use money and not let it use you. If not, you end up not enjoying it."

"..."

"Don't you think so?"

"You're right, my love. You always give me a good lesson. I always end up learning something from you. Who would have thought, right? that in spite of being so young, you're so mature."

"That's right."

"Well, then tell me what you like about me."

"Oh, you already know."

"But tell me anyway."

"You're a nice guy, you're generous, you treat me well, you're sophisticated, you have a good sense of humor— well, *at times*."

"And physically? Do you like the way I look physically?"

"Oh, Santiago, stop asking me so many questions—you're not letting me watch the video."

"Just tell me if you like the way I look, and I promise to stop bothering you. Do you find me attractive?"

"Yeah."

"Do I turn you on?"

"Oh, you know that you do, man. What, you haven't noticed? If I didn't get a hard-on when we fuck, then you could ask me."

"That's fine, my love, I won't bother you any more... Let's keep choosing scenes so we can make a *good* collection with the material from this trip, O.K.?"

"O.K."

3

"Are you asleep?"

"No."

"...I can't sleep. I think I ate too much at dinner... You know what? I think my stomach is a little upset from going overboard so much when we were on vacation..."

"Oh."

"I feel like I'm bloated, like...like I'm constipated. Why don't we go on a diet for a few days?"

"You go on one. My stomach isn't bothering me at all."

"Oh, my love, you could at least support me."

"I hate diets."

"Well, but...all right—I'll go on a diet by myself. I'm going to tell Chabela to include more fiber in my food. Just don't ask to sample what I'm eating."

"O.K."

"That doesn't have to be the case, my love. If you want to, you can ask. Here we do what you desire."

"O.K."

"..."

"Are you worried?"

"No, no, not at all. Why should I be?"

"Because you say you can't sleep."

"Yes, but I already told you why I thought I couldn't."

"You do seem worried to me."

"Why do you say that?"

"Because you've had a worried look on your face for several days now."

"Since when?"

"Since we got back."

"...Maybe I'm a little worried about my health—I haven't been well lately."

"Well, go see a doctor."

"But I don't think it's that big of a deal. I don't think I need to see a doctor right now. I'll be fine once I start my diet—you'll see."

"O.K. I'm going to go to sleep, all right?"

"Yes, my love. Give me a good night kiss."

"Uh-huh."

"Thanks, my love."

"..."

"Now that I'm thinking about it, I believe I am worried about something else."

"Like what?"

"About... Well, I've been thinking it over and...I don't know if I did the right thing by lending that amount of money to..."

"Give me my twenty dollars!"

"I will not—we agreed I'd give you that much every time I mentioned her."

"Exactly."

"But I didn't mention her just now. To mention someone is to say their name."

"Well, you were going to say it. If I didn't cut you off, you were going to say it."

"No, no. I was going to say I don't know if I did the right thing by lending that amount of money to that lady who lives in Mexico City whom you can't stand."

"Well, you were talking about her even though you didn't

say her name."

"Oh, my love, don't be so strict. I need to... Well, I need to talk to you—I need for you to listen to me."

"Don't try to get out of it, Santiago. We had an agreement, didn't we?"

"All right. I'll give you the twenty dollars, but... At least let me tell you about why I'm uneasy, why I'm ..."

"So give me the money."

"Right now?"

"Yeah."

"Oh, my love, you're going to make me get up?"

"Yeah."

"I swear I'll give it to you later. Just let me talk, all right?"

"O.K., but don't pretend you have amnesia later on, got it?"

"No, my love, you know I always keep my word."

"O.K."

"Besides, I'm sure you won't forget."

"Tell me then."

"There's really not much to tell. Just that I've been a little troubled... Well, I don't know if it was a good idea to have lent that money to Sarita."

"Why? Are you running out?"

"No, no, of course not, but... Well, it's a really large sum and..."

"And you're not sure if she's going to repay you."

"Of course not, Arturo. That's not it at all. I have complete trust in Sarita."

"Then? Are you going to have to sell something to be able to keep eating?"

"No, no..."

"Or you're not going to be able to travel anymore?"

"No, that's not it either."

"Then why are you worried?"

"Actually, you're right, my love; the money I loaned to Sarita really won't have any concrete effect on me, but...I don't know—it makes me feel insecure... Well, it's not the same having all your money together as...as having it a little spread out, or as... I'm not wrong, am I?"

"Yes, you are."

"I really don't have any reason to be worried; yet, as you can see, I can't help it. How silly, huh?"

"Uh-huh."

"On the other hand, I should be feeling happy for having helped Sarita."

"Exactly."

"It should satisfy me to know that thanks to me, Sarita is going to be able to start up her own business, and... Well, in a way, I'm contributing to her success, aren't I? And that should make me happy also—the possibility of helping such a beloved friend..."

"Do you think things are going to be all right for her?"

"Of course they are. I don't have any doubt about that. Sarita knows the market very well, and...besides, I'm sure she'll get rid of all her worries in the world."

"Then stop making yourself so nuts. Think about something else."

"You're right, aren't you? Oh, my love, what would I do without you!"

"You would've certainly gone crazy from thinking so much and for thinking about the same thing over and over."

"Why am I like that?"

"I don't know."

"Thank you, my love, for being with me—you don't know how it always helps me to hear your point of view. Talking to you really calms me down—you see things in a more sensible way, more... Well, it's like I was telling you the other day—even though you're very young, you're quite mature. I, on the other hand, feel less secure about things as time goes by..."

"But you're not going to start talking about age, are you?"

"No, my love."

"Do you want something from the kitchen?"

"Are you going downstairs?"

"Yeah, I got hungry. Wouldn't you like something?"

"No, Arturo, I told you that my stomach was a little upset."

"O.K.; go to sleep."

"I'm going to try, my love. I promise I'm going to try to make an effort to sleep. I'm going to do it for you so I don't keep bothering you with my problems. They say insomnia can be contagious."

"But you're not worried any more, are you?"

"No, my love, not anymore."

"O.K. I'll be right back after these messages[14]."

4

"Now take off your pants."

"Uh-huh."

"But don't talk. Concentrate on what you're doing."

"O.K., O.K."

"Just leave your briefs on."

"..."

"Now rub your dick a little bit, like that, gently, barely touching it... Mmmm, that's so hot—you're starting to get hard...that's it, that's it..."

"..."

"...Now put your hand inside your briefs and grab your cock. That's it...take it out."

"..."

"Start playing with it, like you were masturbating. That's it, like that... Close your eyes a minute... Think only about the pleasure you're giving yourself...about how turned on you are."

"..."

"Now turn around and without stopping to play with your dick, pull down your briefs a little bit... That's it... Rub your crack with your other hand... Wow, that's so hot!"

"..."

"Lower your hand a little bit... Like that... Put in between your legs..."

"..."

"Like that... That's so hot!"

"..."

"Don't open your eyes... Like that, like that... Now touch your hole. That's it, that's it...that's so inviting! I'd really like to suck it!"

"..."

"Moisten your lips with your tongue... Slower... That's it, that's it, stick it out a little bit more..."

"..."

"Now lower your briefs until it's around your knees... That's it...and raise up your ass."

"..."

"Like that—what great ass cheeks! What a prize! Stick one of your fingers in your ass."

"..."

"Don't open your eyes, my love... Like that... Stick it in a little bit more... Keep rubbing your dick..."

"..."

"Stick in another finger."

"Two?"

"Don't talk."

"We didn't bring the KY."

"Oh, my love, we agreed you'd be in charge of that."

"I forgot."

"Hold on—I'll go get some. Stay right there."

"You're not going to stop filming?"

"No, it doesn't matter. We'll edit it later... Besides, I want to film some close-ups."

"O.K."

"..."

"..."

"Here you go—take it and lube yourself, but not on camera so no one can see."

"O.K."

"All right, don't talk any more. Let's see... I'm going to take a close-up. Put on your briefs again... Now lower it a little... Like that... And remember with your other hand you were stroking yourself. That's it, like that... Now rub your crack, like that...and put your hand under your briefs... That's it... Caress your crack... That's it..."

"..."

"Now lower your briefs until it's around your knees... Wow, what a sign of things to come! What ass cheeks! Just look! You don't know how hot they look through the lens... Hmmmmm... That's it, my love... Raise your ass a little—like you're offering it to the camera..."

"That's it... That's it..."

"Should I stick in a finger?"

"Yes, but don't talk."

"Oh, Santiago, if you're filming a big close-up of my ass, it doesn't matter if I talk or not."

"Yes, it matters, my love, because you get distracted."

"O.K., O.K."

"...Like that... Stick it in a little more."

"..."

"Like that."

"..."

"That's it!... Now open the KY and lube your hole and the two fingers you're going to stick in."

"..."

"...That's it... That's it... Stick them in slowly at first... Like that... Open up your legs a little bit... Oh yeah, how hot!... That's it... Stick them in a little more..."

"..."

"Does it feel good, you little fucker?"

"Yeah, why don't you come over here and fuck me yourself?"

"That's what you want?"

"Yeah. You have a hard-on?"

"I'm very hard. It's to the point of tearing through my pants... I'm incredibly turned-on."

"Then leave the camera on automatic and fuck me."

"Oh, no, my love—I'm not up for that."

"Why not?"

"I won't look very good... My body will seem horrible compared to yours, so young, so firm..."

"No one is going to see it...or are you going to make a home video?"

"Of course not, but I'm going to see it, which is worse."

"Well, don't get undressed—just take out your cock and fuck me."

"No, no, it would be better if we did that later. In this film, I want it to be only of you...of you enjoying the contact with yourself, with your body, with your fullness... Spread your legs a little bit more."

"O.K."

"That's the way... Well, now I'm going to film a full-shot of the same thing... Take out your fingers and put more KY on them."

"Uh-huh."

"Now stop talking, all right? Pretend I'm not here."

"..."

"...Like that... Really lube yourself up... That's the way... Now stick in your fingers, first slowly and then a little faster, like with more desire... That's it... Stick them in a little bit more, as far as you can... Pant a little bit..."

"No one will be able to hear it—you're talking the whole time."

"We'll dub it later... And stop talking because that is noticeable... Go ahead, pant a little bit... That's it... That's it..."

"..."

"Now with the other hand start rubbing your dick... Like that, that's so hot...jack yourself off... That's it, like that... Faster, faster... Like that... Faster..."

"Oh, I'm about to come."

"Hold on... Try to situate yourself so your cum will fall on your stomach... Turn around a little bit... That's it... Like you were going to sit down... Like that, like that..."

"..."

"..."

"Oh, I'm going to come."

"Come, my love, come... Shoot it all out... Like that, like that...That's it, let it land all over your stomach... That's so hot!"

"..."

"Like that, like that... Now smile with satisfaction and play with your cum. That's the way...Rub it all over your stomach... That's the way... That's the way... How hot!... You do that so well, you little fucker! I'll bet you were a porn star in your former life."

5

"My love, why don't you go downstairs and double check that I turned on the alarm?"

"Oh, no."

"Go ahead. Why is it such a big deal?"

"Yeah, you turned it on. You always turn it on."

"Yes, but now I'm not sure if I really did."

"You always check two or three times. I don't think today is any exception."

"Go ahead, my love... Are you going to make me get up? Keep in mind I'm the one with less energy."

"Don't be obsessive, man. Try to get some sleep."

"So are you going to go?"

"No. I'm going to try to get to sleep, all right?"

"...Fine..."

6

"But what do you want it for, Arturo?"

"What do you mean what do I want it for? Why does anyone want money—to spend it."

"But on what?"

"There are many things I want to buy, that I need."

"Doesn't it seem recently I've been giving you quite a lot?"

"No, it doesn't seem that way."

"Oh, my love, the thing is there's never enough money for you. Really. You're never satisfied—you always want more and more, and that's not good."

"You've always said that money is for that, haven't you? To give yourself happiness and to give it to those around you."

"Yes, but there are limits to everything."

"You said whatever is spent on me is well worth it."

"Yes, my love, but get that look off your face."

"What look?"

"That accusatory look, as if...as if you were about to cry. You do it to try to soften me up, don't you?"

"I'm not about to cry, Santiago."

"Then... I don't know—it's an expression of...it's as if you were sorry for having come to live with me."

"..."

"You think that sometimes, don't you? At times you wonder if you made the right decision to come live here..."

"When you get like that, yeah."

"When I get like how?"

"Like this, when you get super stingy."

"Oh, my love—aren't you being just a little unfair with me?"

"You told me I wouldn't lack for anything, Santiago."

"And do you need something?"

"Yeah, I already told you."

"Oh, my love, it's that you like to buy just for the sake of buying. You don't even need all the things you buy. You have too much of everything—clothes, electronic devices, CD's... You have CD's you haven't even listened to."

"But I'm going to listen to them—you don't have to do everything right away. Are you going to give me the money or not?"

"Oh, Arturo..."

"I do, don't I? I certainly do everything you want—like get buck naked and stick my fingers up my ass so you can film me and jack-off later."

"Hey, listen..."

"Or suck you off in the middle of a highway. And what do I get out of it?"

"Oh, Arturo—don't tell me I force you to do things you don't like to do."

"I'm not saying I don't like doing them, but I'm telling you so you'll see I always try to please you. Remember what you were saying about *pleasing* someone."

"Yes, sure, but...Oh, Arturo, it seems money is the only thing that matters to you."

"It's not the only thing."

"But it's what *most* matters to you, isn't it?"

"*You're* the one who's saying that, huh?"

"..."

"All right—if you don't want to, don't give me anything."

"Oh, my love, don't be like that."

"…"

"How much do you want?"

"Every time I ask you for money we have to argue about it. I'm getting tired of it."

"No, my love—please don't say that. You're making me feel guilty."

"…"

"Forgive me, then. Suddenly I feel…I don't know, insecure about my finances… That's quite a paradox, isn't it? Just when everything seems to be going really well, and I knock on wood nothing goes wrong, I mean, it's strange I feel insecure right now."

"That's what I say."

"But you know we've had a lot of expenses: the trips, the taxes, the car we just bought, the loan to…"

"Aren't you the one who says the more you spend, the more you give, the more you receive?"

"Yes, you're right; I'm wrong. As usual, the person who's wrong is me. Don't pay any attention to me, my love, and forgive me—how much do you need?"

7

"Last night I dreamt I was bankrupt, Arturo—it was horrible... My friends didn't even want to say hello to me—I would go up to them, and they pretended they didn't even know me. And they refused to say 'hi' not because they were afraid someone was going to see them talking to me but because they were scared I was going to ask them for a loan... I got really angry, but I also felt sad and...well, the worst part was I couldn't do anything to get my money back; I could only see how my fortune was disappearing... Oh, no, it was awful..."

"Surely you were going bankrupt because of me, right?"

"No, no, my love—not at all. You weren't even in the dream."

"I had run off with your money!"

"No, I'm telling you that you didn't have anything to do with it."

"Then why were you going broke?"

"I don't know...because of bad investments, because... There were a lot of people who owed me money and who didn't want to pay me—or couldn't. And I had to sell all of my property and... I was still in the red, and... Well, I also owed a lot of money...huge amounts... They were about to put me in jail..."

"What a strange dream."

"All dreams are strange, Arturo."

"Yeah, but some have more to do with what's happening to you in real life than others."

"That's true... Although in actuality it's not such a far-fetched dream."

"Why? Are you on the verge of bankruptcy?"

"No, no, not at all, but I am... Fortunately, it doesn't have to do with my tangible reality—what it has to do with is... Well, with the state of anxiety and of insecurity in which I find myself... It's like I was saying yesterday, isn't it? Who knows why I've been feeling so insecure? It's such a paradox, but that's the way it is... Now, I don't know... Suddenly I have the feeling everyone wants to make a fool out of me."

"Are you saying that because of me?"

"No, no, my love, no."

"Well, I'm the only one who asks you for money."

"Yes, my love, but I'm not talking about that. At least you're up front about asking me for things. I was thinking more along the lines of those...those little tricks of the trade people do to manipulate you—trying to keep you from realizing it, and that's the dirtiest trick: your servants rob you...the mistakes, or the *supposed* mistakes at the restaurants and the stores, the favors people ask you knowing they're trying to defraud you...the abuses of the Internal Revenue Service—all in all...everyone's greed. It's really difficult to conserve your peace and serenity when everyone is trying to figure out how to take advantage of you."

"..."

"But I'm not saying it because of you—is that clear, my love?"

"That's good."

"I don't want you to misunderstand me."

"I assure you I won't, but your constant chattering is really boring, Santiago. You always end up talking about the same thing."

"Listen, that's not true, Arturo. If I..."

"Well, maybe not the same, but you get hung up on a topic, and you don't let it go until you've bored everyone."

"..."

"You're really obsessive, and that gets tiring."

"Are you tired of me?"

"I didn't say that, did I? I'm tired of the way you always repeat everything."

"All right, forgive me. I promise to pay more attention to what I say to you so as not to bore you."

8

"I sometimes think, Arturo, you don't value your relationship with me."

"Why?"

"Or I don't matter to you. Or I matter to you very little—not like you matter to me. Just the other day..."

"Here we go![15]"

"You see, Arturo? For one reason or another, you never let me talk. All of my topics of conversation bother you: my worries, Sarita, money, my health... Nothing that has to do with me is of interest to you."

"It's not that your topics don't interest me, Santiago. What bothers me—and I have already told you this many times—is the way you talk about them: all you ever do is go on and on about something. You're so insistent and obsessive. You simply can't say something once and let it go—that's what I find so boring."

"In that respect I'm realizing you're just like Sarita."

"Pay me!"

"What?"

"You just mentioned her for the second time: forty dollars."

"You see? I'm on the verge of telling you something important, and you come out with one of your jokes."

"It's not a joke, Santiago—we had an agreement."

"Oh, enough, Arturo, please. I'm serious."

"So am I."

"..."

"O.K. What were you going to tell me?"

"..."

"So tell me: why am I just like my mother?"

"That's what Sarita was always like—at least with me. I don't know if she'd be like that with everybody else. When she had a problem, it didn't matter to her at that moment if you weren't in the mood to listen to her—she imposed her need to speak even if it meant ignoring your needs at the time. She always demanded it of you—*she still demands it* of you—an absolute attention to what she's saying."

"Well, I'm *not* just like her, Santiago—I *don't* have problems."

"Think about it, on the other hand whenever you were going to talk to her about something that worried you, she always found a way to trivialize it or avoid it with a joke, with...with an ingenious or supposedly intelligent way out...'I'm really worried, Sarita; I'm having a dilemma.' 'Oh, what can you be worried about, Santiago? You're saying that just to flirt.' And then you could no longer talk because she created a whole theory about you—that having so much money, you couldn't have real problems, that your problems were fantasies you made up to make you look important so others would think you were very complex and...in that sense she was extremely selfish."

"Couldn't it be that you bored her also?"

"No, Arturo. Perhaps I'm too insistent with you because I trust you so much. I trust you like I've never trusted anyone—I can be exactly who I am with you—completely. You are one of the few people whom I can talk to. Just so you know, it doesn't work the same way with Sarita. It's impossible to open up completely with her—you always have the impression she's judging you—that she's too demanding of you—it's almost as if she demands you be someone else—different from who you really are. It's very difficult... That's why it bothers me, my love—that at times you don't want to listen to me."

"All right, what were you going to tell me?"

"About what?"

"Before you began talking about your favorite topic—my mother."

"Well, in fact, I've already told you—at times I get the feeling you don't value your relationship with me."

"And why's that?"

"Because..."

"Come on, don't I do everything you want?"

"Well, yes, but..."

"Or do you think I go around fucking other people?"

No, no, my love—in that respect I don't have any doubts. Thank God."

"Then?"

"Well, because... The other day, for example, when I asked you to make a balance sheet— an evaluation of what the past year had meant for you—it didn't even occur to you to mention your relationship with me—the important things that happened were that you had left home and that...that you had traveled, but not..."

"Oh, Santiago, I didn't mention it because it's obvious. That's understood, isn't it?"

"But you could have said it."

"I hate to be sentimental—you know that."

"Yes, I know, but... At times I need for you to tell me those things, my love. If not... If not, well, if not I'm going to think you're only with me because of my money."

"Stop fucking around with that idea. Enough is enough."

"Tell me my money doesn't matter to you—please, Arturo."

"It would be a lie. Your money does matter to me—a lot, and yeah, money does matter to me—what's wrong with that? Who doesn't like money, Santiago? In fact, I love money. You should accept how I am, and that's that."

"I do accept you, Arturo, but..."

"I accept you. Even though I don't like a lot of your stuff, I accept it, don't I?"

"Yes, my love—thank you."

"So we're not going to talk about this anymore, O.K.? Either accept me as I am, or don't, O.K.?"

"All right, my love—I accept you as you are, but at least tell me you love me."

"Yeah, I love you, Santiago."

"..."

"There you go. Happy?"

"Yes, my love. Thank you."

9

"So how did it go?"

"Fine...fine."

"Do you feel calmer?"

"Uh... Yeah, sure."

"..."

"I think it's what I needed, my love. I felt... I felt a huge relief—it's like the weight of the world is off my shoulders."

"*A lot* of weight[16], dollars actually."

"Really, it was completely cathartic, as they say, even though he hardly spoke, but it helped me a lot anyway."

"Great."

10

"Last night while I was falling asleep I was thinking... Have you ever noticed almost everyone has a fat friend?"

"Uh-huh. Why do you ask?"

"I don't know. I guess it's a kind of... Think about it— almost every group has a similar composition."

"What groups?"

"Groups in general. Social groups... You go to a get-together of people of any age or social class, and you always find either a funny fat man or woman who tells a lot of jokes and who is also the butt of other people's jokes. However uniform or...homogeneous the group is, you always find that kind of fat person."

"That's true, come to think of it."

"Well, and just like there's a fat person in every group, there's also a nervous and insecure skinny person, who never puts on weight because they burn all their energy worrying."

"And a gay person."

"Exactly—a gay person whom you don't always know is gay—someone who may not know it himself—but you also find in every group the sensitive young man with manners that are a bit... refined."

"Oh, Santiago, not all gay people are like that."

"No, no, of course not, my love, especially now when there are fewer...what's the expression? sexual roles. Well, that person doesn't even have to be gay, but in any group you do always find that young guy or older man, don't you?, who's a little delicate and whose manners are a little bit more polished than the rest."

"Uh-huh."

"Well, I was thinking there are always patterns that repeat themselves in whatever group. Models, do you understand? People who...who have a certain type, who are always present...It's like a structure, isn't it? Just like the atom always has a proton, neutron and electron—groups always have certain characteristics."

"And why were you thinking about that?"

"Now you'll see... There's also always a very handsome, seductive young man, like you. And another one who's very assertive, as they say."

"Uh-huh."

"And the only way for things to work right is for each person to fulfill his role—whatever the role is—and without caring if he consciously realizes he's playing a role. For example, if the fat girl goes on a diet and stops being fat, the equilibrium of the group is disrupted. And it's highly probable she'll abandon that group and interact with other people. Therefore, those roles...those roles are what make the groups function—or even society. Think about it...I hadn't. And if you're conscious of your role and if you do everything well, every relationship will be in balance, and then there's nothing more to do. You get a certain feeling of peace, of accepting your destiny, and you stop fighting against the role you get."

"And are you conscious of what your role is?"

"Yes, although I'm not sure if the role chooses you or you choose the role. I still don't know. I really think it's all the same. The important thing is that you fulfill your role."

"And what is your role?"

"Well, when I was thinking about it last night, I realized—at least in my relationship with Sarita—I play the role of something like the idiot friend."

"Oh, Santiago."

"Really. For Sarita, I'm the friend who listens to her, who obeys her will, who does what she wants, who caters to all of her whims and puts up with all of her emotional outbursts who... who is even able to suffer humiliations silently...and who is even a little servile and, on the other hand someone who doesn't judge her or censure her, but who admires her instead and who doesn't ask for anything in return—not even to be listened to or respected."

"..."

"And you know why it's good to have an idiot friend?"

"No, why?"

"...Well, for quite a few reasons, but one of them is it reaffirms your intelligence just like a fat friend reaffirms your slenderness. It's a reference point that allows you to find yourself—a pole. For Sarita, then, I'm useful in that sense, and that's why she tolerates me even though she may think I'm not at her level. It's for that reason and for the concrete advantages she can get from me, don't you think?... Think about it...it suddenly occurs to me all of this was one of her schemes."

"What are you talking about?"

"About... Well, now I can tell you because it doesn't bother me anymore, but for a long time I thought...and I felt really bad. I felt used when I thought Sarita had planned the relationship with you...that everything had been a plan, very carefully thought out and executed, as is Sarita's custom, to see if this poor old idiot would bite."

"You don't have anything to do with being poor."

"Sure. And that's the only thing she was interested in. I even thought it was a plan she and you had put together as co-conspirators."

"Oh, Santiago, you're paranoid."

"Maybe, but paranoid people like me always have a reason

to think the way they do... Since Sarita couldn't marry me, she found the way to establish another bond—maybe a more solid one—using you, without losing the benefits of my friendship."

"Well, even if all that were true, everybody still comes out a winner, right? Isn't that happiness—getting what you want?"

"Exactly, my love. If I were used or manipulated, I'd gladly accept the consequences."

"Well, sure—you have a hot young guy living with you, who you can fuck whenever you want and..."

"Oh, Arturo, you're so cynical in how you say that."

"But that's the way it is, isn't it? Besides, you can introduce me to your friends without getting embarrassed about me; in fact, you even feel proud, don't you?, since I'm handsome and young, and I'm faithful to you."

"Well, yes, my love—you're absolutely right."

"And my mother also ends up winning—sure—because now I'm studying, and I don't ask her for money anymore, so she doesn't have to worry any more. And besides, you lend her money, and she's certain if she had problems, you'd bail her out."

"And you, my love, how did you end up winning?"

"I'm far from my mother, and you give me everything I want although at times it's hard for me to get it out of you."

"That's it?"

"...And I have someone who loves me and who takes care of me without giving me a hard time all the time. You only give me a hard time *some of the time.*"

"You know, at first I was really angry when I realized...certain ways Sarita had taken advantage of me. And when I needed her, she didn't know how to do the same for me. She really infuriated me although I put up with it. But not yesterday—yesterday I could see things very clearly, and I finally understood this was my role life had given me to play—not only with Sarita but in general. Maybe I'm realizing it too late that I'm a goddamn fool, but better late than never, right? You don't know how good it was for me to finally discover this. I felt so calm. For the first time in my life I felt calm. I said—that's how things have to be. It's all right. I'm at peace."

11

"Do you really love me, my love?"

"Yeah, man."

"And are you happy? Completely happy?"

"Yeah, and you?"

"Me too."

12

"Open up wide, little fucker!"

"Ow, it hurts, Santiago."

"I don't believe you—you like it when I push it all the way in."

"Yeah, but it hurts now."

"All right, then, I won't move. Relax."

"Uh-huh."

"Think about something else."

"What?"

"I don't know...something else...how about the present I'm going to give you for your birthday for example. Do you know what you want yet?"

"Yeah."

"What?"

"I'm not going to tell you right now."

"But you're less tense now, aren't you, you little fucker?"

"Uh-huh."

"I can't imagine what it is you want, but I'm sure you're going to break me."

"There's something to that."

"..."

"..."

"Are you enjoying this?"

"Yeah, a lot."

"You're such a little fag, aren't you?"

"Yeah... Oh, that's it, Santiago...fuck me harder! Like that! That's it!"

"But stop moving so much, Arturo—we're going to be out of the range of the camera."

Cuernavaca, February 1991—February 1993

Endnotes

[1] Translator's Note: In Spanish, by adding the suffix –ita to a person's name—in this case Sara—the speaker wishes to convey a sense of endearment.

[2] Translator's Note: Spanish divides all nouns into grammatical categories of masculine and feminine gender. Nouns that end in the letter "o" are often masculine while nouns that end in the letter "a" are often feminine. Here Arturo makes fun of Santiago by changing his gender and addressing him as if he were a woman.

[3] Translator's Note: Lomas is the name of an area in Mexico City where wealthy people reside.

[4] Translator's Note: The Zona Rosa is an area in Mexico City that caters to tourists. It offers many restaurants, bars, clubs, cafés, bookstores as well as shopping. The Zona Rosa is also popular with gays and lesbians.

[5] Translator's Note: Sanborns is a chain of restaurants throughout much of Mexico City. It is similar to a Denny's in the United States.

[6] Translator's Note: Chapultepec is a neighborhood in Mexico City where upper middle-class Mexicans live. It is also the area where the Chapultepec Park and Zoo are located.

[7] Translator's Note: This line appears in English in the original. Santiago worries someone may hear what they say in Spanish

and decides to use English.

8 Translator's Note: Santiago and Arturo continue their conversation in English for the next nine lines in the original text.

9 Translator's Note: At this point Santiago and Arturo revert back to speaking in Spanish in the original text.

10 Translator's Note: Arturo is punning on the word *principios*, which in Spanish has two meanings. It can mean "principles" as Santiago says three lines earlier. It can also mean, however, "beginnings." Here Arturo subverts Santiago's seriousness with his ability to pun.

11 Translator's Note: Valle de Bravo is a town in the state of Mexico with a lake where wealthy Mexicans have weekend homes.

12 Translator's Note: This line appears in English in the original text.

13 Translator's Note: Arturo is punning on the word *inconsciente*, which in Spanish can mean "an irresponsible or inconsiderate person" or "unconscious."

14 Translator's Note: This line appears in English in the original text.

15 Translator's Note: This line appears in English in the original text.

16 Translator's Note: Arturo is punning on the word *peso*, which in Spanish can mean "weight" or "the national currency of Mexico."

Printed in the United States
53735LVS00001B/1-9